His Second Chance #2

His Pirate

By Stephanie Lake

Enjoy Rhain's Story!

Steph

& Lake

eXcessica publishing

Second Chance 2: His Pirate © May 2017 by Stephanie Lake

Excessica LLC
P.O. Box 127
Alpena, MI 49707

To order additional copies of this book, contact:
books@excessica.com
www.excessica.com

First Edition by Loose Id May 2017
Cover design Originally by April Martinez
Originally edited by Keren Reed

Dedication

To our fans, who make writing worth the time, toil, rewrites, and more rewrites! Hugs!!!

Acknowledgment

Thanks to our fantastic beta readers, Jules Radcliffe, Mae Hancock, and Autumn Montague. Special thanks go to our patient and ever so tactful editor, Keren Reed. Cheers to April Martinez for another fantastic cover.

Chapter One

London, August 1809

The man was the ideal male specimen, except for the frown. Well, the frown and the nose. The nose a bit too prominent, a bit too hooked to be considered perfect, but it was a fully male-manly nose, which saved the face from a lack of character. Sleek brown brows over eyes the color of…of what? Damn the lighting in the Red Pig's taproom; he couldn't tell what color they were, but they were dark.

And those lips. They were full but smooth, not puffy like some. Puffy lips always looked like an over-yeasted pastry. But these lips were perfect for sliding a kiss onto.

Rubbing the engraved gold clasp securing the thin braid that fell over his ear, Captain Alastair Breckenridge leaned against the taproom's door frame and let the door close. The sound of sea birds immediately turned to muffled cries. He allowed his eyes to adjust after the murky sunlight and took a moment to fully admire the man. Conservative but expensive clothing. Brown on brown over tan. He might be the boring type, dressing so drably. But really, who would care so long as they were grasping shoulders so broad as to eclipse the moon?

God. He obviously needed a good fuck in order to concentrate on finding cargo and stop envisioning acts that would not happen in this seedy tavern, in this seedy part of town, and certainly not with a man who glowers.

The room was only half-full. Midafternoon was not a popular drinking hour. Even so, two drunks in the corner made more noise than a squabbling family of ten laborers. The warm, humid air reeked of sour ale and cabbage, which was preferable to the stench of unwashed bodies that would permeate the tavern in a few hours when it filled.

Alastair closed his eyes and imagined what the man with the scowl would smell like. Fresh and sweet, that was obvious from his clean appearance. But what would be under the starch and soap? Would he smell like the forest, fresh earth, the air right before a storm? Hopefully he would not smell like the sea. Everyone he'd taken to bed the past few months smelled like brine, a scent that got tiresome very quickly.

Unable to ignore the glowering man who sat at a table alone, looking out of place, he finished his assessment: A mostly full tankard of ale close by his elbow. Must not be used to such unrefined fare. The man's chin was strong but not overly so. Clean-shaven, pale skin. In total, a handsome package. He would have approached the man, introduced himself, tried to improve the young man's mood—if not for creased skin between brows and across his forehead that tattled about this man's temperament. Not a jovial youth to be certain. And Alastair did not associate with troubled people.

Better to look elsewhere for companionship tonight.

He would ask the barkeeper if anyone inquired about a ship heading west. They lost their contracted cargo because of the damn two-month delay returning to London and would likely lose the regular loads along the way as well. Damn the Moroccan government's impound laws. Two months his ship sat waiting for him to grease the correct palms with an ungodly amount of money. He must pick up more cargo to make the sail profitable.

The barkeeper had worked at this seedy establishment for at least a decade, about as long as Alastair captained the *Hurricane*. The man was straight-dealing, with a good memory. That's why Alastair kept coming here for tips on who needed what cargo shipped around the world.

Pushing away from the doorjamb, he caught the barkeeper's attention and strode to the bar. "Hear of any cargo, One Eye?" No one had ever been brave enough to ask how the hulking brute lost his right eye. Not that he'd heard, anyway.

The man nodded and pointed.

Alastair turned in time to catch the handsome, sulking youth stare right at his arse before that gaze snapped to his face.

Well, well, well. His afternoon had just gotten exponentially more complicated and *much* more interesting.

BY GOD, HE was beautiful—in a strange sort of way.

At first Rhain Morgan thought the graceful person lounging in the door frame was a very athletic woman in costume. Perhaps the entertainment for the afternoon, dressed in a billowy shirt and tall boots. But as soon as the pirate crossed the room, he knew that lethal stalking, the firm bunch and release of muscles, could only belong to a man. A man in his prime and in prime condition. Fighting condition.

A true to life swashbuckler, then. A pirate in the blood and flesh, here in London of all places. Rhain had never seen one before, so he was surprised a pirate could be so…well, unmarred and attractive. The satires always portrayed men of the sea as ragged, dirty, with most of their fingers missing, or worse.

Months had passed since he'd desired a man. He thought those unnatural desires were mostly conquered, but this man with his swagger and confidence sent a tingle of interest to his groin. Damn, and he'd been thinking it was time to put his youthful follies behind him, marry, beget an heir.

Good God, this man and the way he moved. Graceful and sinewy.

One thing for certain, the pirate was not here for anyone's entertainment. More like some mayhem was afoot.

Time to leave.

Coming here and spending half a day with bad food and even worse ale had been a mistake. Not only did he *not* find a ship to take him and his precious cargo to Dominica, now he would have erotic dreams for months, if not longer, about this stunning man.

The pirate leaned over to speak to someone at the bar. Slim hips and a firm backside with a tempting narrowing of the waist, the flawless form so few men possessed. Since that backside was covered by tight tan breeches and accentuated with a wide burgundy leather belt, he knew he would see very little sleep this night. But that wasn't the worst part. At that moment, the barkeeper pointed to him, and the pirate turned, snapping obsidian-black eyes his direction.

Bloody hell! Too late to make an escape.

He forced his shoulders to relax and tried to look unconcerned as he slipped the dagger from his boot.

"I heard you want to hire a ship. I happen to have one." The pirate sat down with a slow, deliberate slide across the table from him without an invitation. "Captain Breckenridge of the *Hurricane*." He spoke properly and nodded politely, the pleasantry so out of character with the picture the captain presented, Rhain thought the man perhaps mocked his upper-class bearing and attire.

"The cost is eight hundred pounds for a direct route and immediate departure to Dominica, which includes wages for the crew. We can leave as soon as the crew is rounded up." His voice was a smooth, silky tenor. The type of voice that could lull you to sleep even as your throat was cut. A voice so soothing, he almost agreed with the price before registering it was open-seas robbery.

"Eight hundred pounds? You must be mad. I assure you my sister and I do not require champagne and caviar each night."

"It is late for a westerly crossing. You are not likely to find another ship at this date."

Yes, Rhain had been told that by many captains going the opposite direction. And he couldn't wait. Lydia's condition worsened with each passing day. If she improved away from the cold, wet weather and smog, then his conviction that she did not have tuberculosis would be proven. This boat was his last chance to save his little sister. A tight band squeezed around his chest, and he fought to relax and take a deep breath.

"Why, then, are you going westward?"

"We were held up in customs for two months on my last leg. Cost me a small bag of silver to bribe all the people involved in releasing my ship with its cargo. So we are late for our regular route. I've been contemplating missing a year of our Atlantic crossing, but if I can obtain the right load, we will make the journey."

Rhain argued, and for a half hour they negotiated a lower price and, unfortunately, a delayed departure so the captain had time to find cargo. Drawn to the pirate's curly, jet-black hair, Rhain's attention floundered, making it impossible to concentrate on how each additional stop would decrease the price but increase the time it took to arrive at his plantation in Dominica. The pirate wore his hair pulled back by a band at his nape, except for one flirty thin braid by his right ear, which slipped back and forth over his shoulder as he moved. Even more distracting was the way he would occasionally move one long, ropy-muscled arm to twist a gold ring in one perfect ear, the blousy sleeve slipping to his elbow. Then he was just as likely to run an elegant finger across a groove in the scarred table.

Despite everything, they finally agreed on a price, although it would nearly wipe out his savings and delay their arrival by an extra two or more weeks, depending on how quickly the pirate obtained the requisite cargo and how many stops were needed to deliver the cargo.

Having come to an agreement, Rhain's worry grew. Would it be safe to sail with this man and his crew?

"Just how old are you? You don't look old enough to captain a ship."

The pirate pulled himself up from a half sprawl on the table, his movements slow and predatory. "I am one and thirty, sir, and a damn fine captain. My father wanted me to learn to sail properly, so he stuffed me on a government ship. The HBMS *Dragon* captained by Lord Wentworth. A bloody viscount of all things, but he is one of the damn finest captains I have ever seen. I learned as much as I could in those four years, then worked on one of my father's ships. I started as acting captain on the *Hurricane* at one and twenty and gained ownership of her at five and twenty." One could tell he was proud of his accomplishments by the rapid speech and lift in his voice.

Rhain found he believed this man to be a good captain. A man capable of sailing to Dominica.

His pulse pounded at his temples. Lydia would survive after all. Once he got her out of this hellhole and to a hot, smogless locale, she would be fine. This pirate, or captain as he called himself, would do that for them.

He'd sold everything but a few crates of possessions to pay for their travel, then sold their small home to pay for what they would need in Dominica, so he and Lydia were ready to leave. He was not happy over the delay to ship out, but he could not afford to rent the entire damn vessel.

He examined the man across the table. Really looked at him—at the hungry ebony eyes and his do-what-is-needed-to-earn-a-bag-of-gold stare—and his doubts came tumbling back. They would not make it in time for Lydia. Or worse, this man would take them to the deepest part of the ocean, dump them overboard, and then sell their goods and keep all profits without a blink of those thick-lashed eyes. For God's sake, it looked as though he had applied kohl around his eyes to enhance the intensity of that stare.

He took a deep breath to calm his fears. Perhaps the worst that would come of their crossing was this rekindling of his need to visit molly houses. He sighed and stood to leave.

The pirate grabbed him with a strong, work-roughened but elegant hand.

The feel of those long fingers on his wrist froze him to the spot and sent longing through his arm to his whole body.

"When our holds are full, we will leave with the retreating tide. Depending on the day, this could be early morning. I will send you notice the evening before departure. Is that enough time for you to prepare and have all your cargo at the dock before six of the clock?"

Rhain nodded, scrawled his address with some apprehension, and left the dark, noisy tavern with his damn rod at half-mast and his dagger up a sleeve at the ready.

Chapter Two

Rhain took one last look at the small, soot-stained boarding house he and Lydia had lived in the past month. It had been necessary to find a modest place to stay while finalizing the sale of their mother's small London home.

God, but it would be good to leave London and these dreary rented rooms with their even drearier landlady, Mrs. Prescott, who always complained Lydia's coughing kept her up at night.

Leaving the home he grew up in had been much more difficult. The home where his mother's presence could still be felt, even after she passed away when he was only six. This place felt like a part of him. He'd always thought he would live out the rest of his days surrounded by its dark-paneled walls. Signing the papers to hand over ownership had been one of the most difficult things he hoped to ever face.

From some silly sentiment, he'd gone back to see the brick building one last time, yesterday. Remembering all the love he, his sister, and Father shared in that place until Father passed, some... He counted back. Six years ago.

Since then he'd acted as head of his and Lydia's little family.

Walking back to their sad set of rented rooms after seeing the home he'd loved from childhood, his eyes had been moist. He'd felt ridiculously melancholy.

"Come now, Rhain," Lydia said, jerking his attention back to the present and their current adventure. She looked at him wide-eyed. "We don't want to risk missing the boat."

He smiled at her. God, so good to see her excited about something for a change. Ever since he'd told her they would leave London, she'd spun stories about all the adventures they would have on their voyage and at their plantation, which she now called their island paradise. Some of these stories involved handsome men in blue sweeping her off her feet with romance, even though he repeatedly told her they were not traveling on a military vessel. Other stories involved how they would never utilize slaves and would convince the island government to abolish slavery on their island.

He climbed into the wagon he'd hired to carry all their worldly possessions to the docks.

The driver smacked the rump of two scrawny horses with the reins, and the wagon jerked forward with creaks and groans.

They were clattering over cobblestones, not twelve yards away, when Lydia started in on another adventure story.

Rhain laughed, enjoying her exuberance. "Let me assure you, dear girl. The ship we will sail on is not romantic. It is barely more than a pirate vessel. In fact, the captain looks more like a pirate who should be brandishing a cutlass rather than captaining a ship." He proceeded to describe the stunning man, down to whipcord strong body and that flirty braid.

"Oh, he sounds marvelously wicked." She gave him an impish grin. "Then perhaps we will be rescued by a Royal Navy ship with hundreds of sweet-faced lieutenants missing home and romantic company."

"Lydia!"

Her light laughter turned into a racking cough.

His chest tightened at the sound. He glared at the foul London air, the combination of smoke and fog that made her condition so much worse, and wished they were on the damn floating transport already. The week and a half wait between agreeing on a price and setting sail had been excruciating. Twice in that time, Lydia was overcome with fever. He felt so helpless when she succumbed to her illness; just thinking about it made him want to grab the reins from the driver's hands and stir the horses into a dash to get her out of the poor air now.

To take Lydia's mind off her coughing fit, he said, "The captain might remind you of a disreputable pirate, but not to worry, I have it on the best authority that he runs a tight ship."

Rhain investigated the pirate during the excruciatingly long week and a half it took the man to provision his ship. The pirate had a good reputation, which put Rhain at ease with his decision to whisk his sister away from the only home they had ever known.

Away to some place they had never seen, a place halfway around the world.

* * * *

Alastair pulled on his leather greatcoat to fight the sharp morning wind blowing in from the North Sea and watched the brooding young man help his fragile sister along the dock toward the *Hurricane*. The two appeared nothing alike. She was waifish, hesitant, with a head full of white-blonde hair that fell into ringlets around a pretty, heart-shaped face and with eyes so blue, he could tell their hue from the quarterdeck.

Her brother, in contrast, was big—large boned, tall; shoulders that looked like they could carry the world and likely often did. His rich brown hair was short and straight, and Alastair knew from their brief meeting the previous night that his eyes were a stimulating whiskey brown.

He'd dreamed of those eyes last night. Although most of the dream evaporated upon waking, he remembered a gaze full of desire.

"I have a bad feeling about this, Dunn," he confessed to his first mate.

"Aye, sir, and why is that? They look like a fine family coming aboard."

"Yes, but the girl is very ill with something, and Morgan was unable to convince me it is not consumption."

First Mate Conall Dunn gripped the bulwark cap until white-knuckled. "Why did you invite them aboard, sir?"

"She is not contagious, I was assured, and we need the fare, so I took the risk that the boy is telling the truth." Alastair sighed and ran a finger over the grooves in his gold hair clasp. "Their fare will help pay for some of the bribe moneys we spent getting the *Hurricane* out of Morocco, and depositing them on their island will not be far out of our way."

Knuckles still white, Dunn spat over the side. "Damn worthless country, in my opinion. Can't believe we're going back there." At Alastair's glare, he said, "'Course, you found us cargo, so guess we should be thankful of that, and now we know how to avoid the customs men." He kept watching their passengers as they neared the ship. "Such a sweet-looking girl. Should not have to suffer such."

"Hmm, maybe, but if she takes after her brother, she is not going to be sweet-natured. She will be a firebrand. Uncontrollably feisty." His lips threatened to smile just from talking about Mr. Rhain Morgan. He fought the absurd reaction, but for some reason he could not stop thinking about his two brief interactions with the young man. Once at the Red Pig and then last night to inform him they would sail today.

He could have sent one of his crew to inform Morgan of their departure, but he'd wanted to see the man again. Morgan had been in shirtsleeves, his hair rumpled as if from hours of messing it with his hands.

Only allowed several steps past the entry door of cheap rented rooms, Alastair did not feel welcome. There was faint coughing behind a closed door off to one side of the small main room, and Morgan acted as if Alastair had purposefully delayed the departure date. The meeting had not been as pleasant as he had hoped, but there was enough light to enjoy the sight of linen-covered broad shoulders and whiskey-colored eyes.

"Suppose they will be accepting with the goings-on of some of the crew?"

"We should probably give instructions to restrict the interesting activity to secluded corners belowdeck."

"Crew won't like that; they sign on because of the freedom they have on board."

He only nodded. This would be an interesting sail at best, a catastrophe at worst. He should have doubled the fee.

He watched the big man help his sister over a broken crate spilled out over the dock. Turning at Dunn's sigh, he watched the normally stoic first mate lean against the bulwark as if that move alone could help the girl safely to the ship.

"Stop being all moony-eyed over that girl. You falling for the gent's sister will ensure our voyage is a disaster."

Dunn bristled. "Yes, well, with all due respect, make sure to keep your prick in your drawers too, sir."

Shocked beyond words, he watched his first mate step away from the bulwark and go about his business.

Had Alastair been that obvious with his attraction? Probably.

Yes, he had a bad feeling about this voyage. Yes, indeed!

* * * *

With everything stowed, the *Hurricane* was unmoored and slipped away from the pier, floating out of the harbor and then downstream toward the North Sea. They would sail close to shore until reaching the Channel. As usual, the crew effortlessly trimmed the ship, unfurling, raising, and securing sails.

To protect against French attacks, they traveled with a contingent of Navy and other private vessels. Some ships would go their separate way as they traveled, and after Lisbon, the *Hurricane* would journey alone. With about thirty ships in their group, the Thames was too crowded at this point to run at full sail, but the fleet would be ready once the river widened and they hit the estuaries.

Alastair loved this part of the trip—the anticipation of a new voyage, leaving the stench of a port town, the feel of his ship slicing through the water, taking him and his crew and cargo to wherever he wished to go. Nothing but the weather and the sea dictating what they could and could not do.

Thinking about what he'd like to do just then, he decided to seek out his new passengers.

Morgan fussed with the ropes, securing his meager possessions. His sister stood at the bulwark, gaping at the view of the summer-green river bank.

"First time on an ocean-going vessel, Miss Morgan?"

She looked over at him, and if it were possible, her wide blue eyes doubled in size. "You do look... Umm, just like Rhain said you did." She put a petite gloved hand over her mouth. "Pardon my rudeness, Captain, but from his description, I would have recognized you anywhere."

"Is that so? Should I be flattered or worried?"

She smiled but avoided his question. "Actually, this is my first time on anything bigger than a row boat." She waved toward the river, which grew larger and wider as they navigated downstream. "It is so verdant and lush, and the air is already cleaner. I feel lightheaded from all the fresh air."

The outline of her profile showed a slight resemblance to her brother. That stubborn chin and light freckling on her nose, but that was all, the rest too feminine to remind him of Morgan.

The girl turned and gave him a frank gaze. "I do appreciate you taking us on, Captain." She held out a hand, and he took it carefully, afraid anything more than a light squeeze would break her birdlike fingers.

"I assure you, Miss Morgan, your brother paid me a fair sum, and no thanks are necessary." Actually, her brother paid a king's ransom for this trip, but Alastair would not freely offer that information. "There are not many ships going to the Caribbee Islands this time of year due to weather. Your brother was lucky to find us before I had cargo and headed to Constantinople."

She clasped her hands as if in glee. "Will we see any thrilling storms, do you think?"

The girl must be daft to excite over the possibility. Well, might as well give her something to look forward to. "Yes, I imagine we will, miss. But not to worry. I have a first-class crew."

"I'm certain you do, sir." She smiled at him and then turned to cover a horrible, racking cough with an embroidered handkerchief.

"Shall I alert your brother?"

She shook her head and waved him on. "No, no, I'll be fine..." She coughed again. "In a few moments."

"With your leave." He bowed but doubted she saw him in her bent-over position, one hand on the bulwark cap keeping her thin frame from slumping to the main deck.

He found Morgan leaning across one crate to test the integrity of a board on another, firm thighs and muscular arse pointing right at him.

Mother of God, what a sweet sight. He wanted so much to run his fingers up those firm thighs, feel the hard muscles under the worn, rough wool. Instead he waited until the man stood and Alastair asked, "Will it hold, or should I bring a crewman to shore it up?"

The man turned to appraise him. This was the first time they'd spoken since last night, and what a vision he was up close and in full daylight. His strong, sculpted lips shouted "kiss me;" his strong chin suggested the hint of a cleft when he wasn't sporting a half-day beard. In the drab brown coat and pale-yellow shirt, he could be a clerk, but Alastair knew he was of gentle birth, for his accent spoke of the aristocracy. A third cousin to a baron perhaps, whose family lost all their money to gambling or bad investments? Alastair didn't know, but there awaited a long journey in which to find out. And he planned to, because this man interested him.

"No, the boards seem sound enough," Morgan said in his rumbling baritone. He tapped the crate lovingly. "This was my mother's pianoforte, so I made certain it was secured properly."

"Do you play?"

Morgan nodded and patted the crate again. "And my sister plays the harp. We have wasted many evenings in the frivolous pursuit of music, I'm afraid. Do you play a musical instrument, Captain?"

He checked his almost routine answer—"I'm an expert at playing the rod"—because this man was not one of his crude, seen-everything-and-done-most-of-it-too crew. He said instead, "No, but I enjoy listening. I've asked Swanson here"—he pointed to a man with skin such a rich black it appeared deep sapphire in dim lighting—"to show you and your sister to your quarters. Lunch will be served at two and supper at seven. Swanson will show you where the galley is. If you are feeling unable to eat, as so many do once the ship starts to sway, let someone know, and cook can make you a draught of weak salted beer. It does wonders for a foul stomach."

Morgan blanched at the mention of the cocktail.

"Here is how I estimate our journey to go. The weather is in our favor for now, so we will make good time on the outset, but I picked up four commissions for delivery since we met Wednesday last, and we will have to make two additional stops, putting our arrival to Dominica perhaps three months from now."

The young man looked at his sister, still doubled over in a coughing fit. "Further delays."

The news did not apparently go down well, since the young man fairly shook with rage, fists clenched and teeth grinding. He really did need to practice hiding—if not controlling—his anger. Otherwise he would die of apoplexy.

"My dear sir, do you need a drink?"

"No, I do not need a drink in the middle of the day," Morgan spat the words out between clenched teeth. "What I need is a captain who will give me an honest estimate. You know I have a frail sister who needs warmer climes to improve her health, and we have already waited almost two weeks. You originally assured me it would be four fortnights at the longest, depending on the location of your cargo deliveries."

"Indeed, that was the plan I had when we met before. However, this is a working ship that makes money from delivering cargo and buying and selling goods. We have additional cargo now, thus the need for a few more, very short stops." He found his voice rising, when normally he became slow and cold during arguments. There was something about the boy's high color and prickly nature that made him want to roil Morgan.

"How dare you not inform me as soon as you changed your plans? I could have—"

"Could have what? Found a different ship going to Dominica this time of year?" He took two steps closer to Morgan, who stiffened but didn't back down. Bravo for the boy.

This was the first time he stood close enough to realize Morgan was several inches the taller. He liked that. Liked that a lot. Not many men were taller than him, and the boy's bulk would feel wonderful pushing him into a mattress. But there were better times than this to think of fucking an irate passenger.

Straightening his shoulders to act like a proper captain, he said, "I command this vessel and will not allow insubordination from my crew or my passengers. You are already committed to the journey, and one or two weeks here or there will make no difference. So I suggest, to make this trip more comfortable for yourself, you improve your attitude."

"Or else?"

Or else, I might just kiss those sculpted lips of yours until you melt in my arms. He took one half step closer. So close, he could see two whiskers that escaped the morning razor. "Or else, you will spend the rest of the journey in a skiff tied to the back of the ship. Not a very comfortable ride, on that you may rest assured." Then he moved that last half step forward so that their bodies touched, and ran a finger down Morgan's chest under his simply tied cravat. The flesh under the summer-weight linen felt firm and warm.

"There is no need to attempt to intimidate me, sir. I assure you it will not work." The boy's lips pursed as if fighting off a scowl, or perhaps a smile, because that fine body shivered.

Good sign. Very good.

Alastair bit his tongue to keep from laughing at the proud boy. "Not to worry, Mr. Morgan. Intimidating you is the last thing on my mind right now."

He casually brushed their crotches together as if by accident and enjoyed the boy's response. Wide eyes, slack jaw, and a soft, drawn-in breath.

For two thundering heartbeats he enjoyed the man's flushed face, then turned away and ordered his crew to set his ship to full sail.

Chapter Three

As Swanson walked by, Lydia's head turned. Was she tracking him? The man stopped and looked boldly at her.

"Have you never seen black skin before, miss?" he asked.

Lydia blushed. "Why, no. I'm sorry, I know it's ill-mannered to stare. But I find it so fascinating!"

Swanson laughed, his teeth gleaming very white in his black face. "Would you like to touch it?"

"May I?" Her voice was filled with wonder.

"Lydia!"

His sister jumped at the rebuke, but Swanson only maintained his wide smile and nodded.

"Aye, miss. The first time I saw white people, I could not believe skin could be such a strange color! I had to touch it to make sure it was real." He held out a muscled, tight-skinned arm, glistening ebony.

Lydia looked over her shoulder as if to ask Rhain for permission. He rolled his eyes—Lydia was not to be stopped, she had always been inquisitive. Reaching out a slender finger, she tentatively touched and then rubbed the man's arm.

Beaming up at the sailor, she said, "It feels just like my skin."

"Yes, miss, all's the same under the first layer." The sailor winked cheekily at his sister, and the chit giggled up at him.

He was going to have a difficult time keeping her in check and safe on this longer-than-expected voyage. He sighed. "Can we see our rooms please?"

"As you wish, sir."

They were shown down a narrow, low-ceilinged passage paneled in unfinished light-colored wood. Swanson opened two doors, side by side, and launched Lydia's portmanteau onto a tiny berth in the first room. "Here be your quarters. Fancy as can be found on the *Hurricane*." He winked and hurried off to other duties.

Lydia, hand over her mouth, murmured, "So small, Rhain. I just might suffocate in here."

The room was bare save for the berth. Pale wooden walls were barely wider than Rhain's shoulders one direction and likely shorter than his full length the other direction. Little light streamed through the extremely small and stained round window.

He put his hand on her shoulder, knowing that with her hampered breathing, she hated feeling confined. "Most of the time we will be walking around up top. This is just for sleeping, and if we must, we will figure out a way to safely sleep with our doors ajar. Don't worry."

She nodded but did not look at all impressed. "How long did you say this trip would take? Three fortnights?"

"Now it will be longer, possibly three months, hopefully no more than that. I admit I was perhaps overly optimistic when I heard the original estimate, and concentrated on the shortest possible interval." Or perhaps he'd been concentrating on that flirty braid and did not hear the entire conversation.

"Lydia, I wish the trip were shorter. I hope you will be able to sleep with all this popping, creaking, and groaning. I had no idea a boat would make so much noise."

She nodded. "And so much swaying." Peering around the opening into the tiny room, she said, "The ship seemed so big and cheerful from the outside, with its dark varnished wood and bloodred stripe. I didn't expect such a small, austere place to sleep. I don't think Mother would ever have done something like this."

"Of course not; she was raised to be very refined. Father on the other hand, I think, had he not fallen in love with Mother and then been forced to take care of two children, would have loved the adventure."

"Well, then, let us have his adventure for him, shall we?" With that she threw her thin shoulders back and stepped into the stuffy little room.

* * * *

Two days into the trip and Alastair tired of watching Dunn stare lovelorn at Miss Lydia—as the young woman insisted on being called. Most of this resentment came about because he knew good and well he acted just as lovesick over Mr. Morgan. In fact, a dozen or so of the crew gawked at that big bonny body as he walked about ship.

The boy could have fucked most of the crew if he crooked a finger. At least, any man not committed. Hell and damnation, even half the matelots watched this powerful man, but Morgan did not seem to realize. His attention was always on his sister.

What a mess he'd gotten himself into. He couldn't sleep for fantasizing about the robust youth, so how could he in good conscience chastise Dunn for his infatuation with such a vibrant young lady?

And she was vibrant.

Amazing how, in just two days, she turned from a weak girl who coughed much of the time into an adventurer, an educator, and someone with such a lust for life. Everyone on ship wanted to be in her presence.

Morgan, it seemed, noticed the attention and would not stray more than ten feet from her side.

Alastair didn't blame him. That girl was destined to do something outside of propriety. She embraced new experiences and enjoyed all the differences she experienced. If she were his sister, he'd lock her belowdeck and not let her out without a chastity belt.

Currently, Morgan leaned against the bulwark and read, or pretended to read, a book, while Lydia taught eighteen of his toughest sailors the alphabet and how to spell simple words. She was a marvel, the way she convinced the seamen that reading would improve their lot in life and kept their interest during the class with stories.

Alastair would love to keep her. The crew, always loyal because of their freedom on his ship, would likely start paying to work for him since they received an education, and entertainment to boot, with Miss Lydia teaching them and singing between times.

He'd not heard her cough more than once or twice since the Channel merged with the ocean. Not surprising. The ocean air was so much fresher than the smoke-and-fog-choked London. He never understood why Mother was determined to stay there. Of course, her four or five lovers and three bastard children might have something to do with it, but still. With her looks, even at fifty, and the money she inherited from her bachelor brother, she could move anywhere.

For what must have been the twentieth time that morning, his gaze veered to the man haunting his dreams of late. Morgan, relaxed enough to go without a cravat today, leaned against the bulwark. He held the small book loosely in one hand and tilted his head back, eyes closed, gathering sun rays on his face. He reminded Alastair of a wolfhound lazing on a sunny step. If he kept this up, that sprinkling of freckles would turn into a lickable freckle map across his face.

Alastair shook that thought away. Even so, it was difficult to pull his gaze away from such an entrancing sight, but he would not be caught moon gazing like Dunn. In fact, he should put a stop to that right now, before he talked with Morgan.

Dunn leaned over the quarterdeck, chin on fist, staring at Lydia with a puppy-like, worshipful expression.

He walked up the stairs, across the scrubbed boards, and then knocked one knee out from under his first mate.

"What the…" The man came up swinging, and Alastair readied for a fight.

Dunn pulled his punch before hitting his captain. "What the bloody 'ell'd you do that for?"

"You were completely unaware of your surroundings. I could have cut your throat."

"No, sir, I—"

"Yes, I could have. It is one thing to admire a fine figure, but don't neglect your duty to this ship while dreaming about getting your nose under that skirt."

"But, sir—"

"No. Listen to me, and this time pay attention. That woman is quality, and you are the second son of a washerwoman. No matter that you managed to educate yourself, you are not in her class and never will be. And if you continue to neglect your duties, I will find myself a new first mate."

Dunn bristled. Mouth in a snarl, he looked away before his anger took over. He was a good first mate and knew his place.

Alastair moved in close and whispered, "I will not allow you to ruin her reputation or her chastity. Do I make myself clear?"

"Yes, sir. But I would never—"

"I expect you to tell the rest of the crew that they will protect her and not harm her in any way. Is that also clear?"

"Yes, of course. Captain, you know I wouldn't. We've been friends—"

Alastair glared at him.

"…working together for five years. You know you can trust me."

Alastair gave him one of his cold smiles he knew made his crew's skin crawl. "Make sure I don't regret putting my trust in you, then."

Rising to his full height, which fell somewhere around short, Dunn squared his shoulders and gave a sloppy salute.

He almost laughed at the man's indignant anger over a slip of a girl but instead stopped the man from leaving angry. "You know what an awful idea it is to have an affair with quality. Especially someone you will leave in a port and never see again."

"Aye, sir, I am quite aware. But I can't help wondering why you keep staring at Mr. Morgan. Perhaps you should take your own advice."

Alastair paused, feeling the smooth ridges on his braid clasp to give himself time to think. Why did he keep staring at Morgan? The boy was handsome, true, but that had never been enough to hold his attention for long. He was prickly, yes. He was a challenge, most definitely. Was that enough to justify this fascination? Something for him to think about. Until then he would prevaricate. "Things are different for me, you know that, Dunn. Even if we share an interest, Mr. Morgan and I can have no future together, no matter what happens."

His first mate nodded and then looked out at the water. "Your father will not be happy knowing you picked up a couple of nobs, seeing as how he disagrees with the way you run your ship; won't want word getting out there are credible witnesses who can confirm you let your crew commit buggery. He might take this ship away from you, not realizing you made the crew behave on this trip."

Alastair's gut tightened, hearing someone else state his recurring fear. "With any luck, Father will never find out."

He swallowed. Hard. Trying to force away the memory not too many years past, of a late night, too much brandy, and an uncomfortable discussion with his father. *"I know you let your scum of a crew fornicate in plain view, but what about you? Do you dip your wick in men as well?"*

Alastair shot back. *"What does it matter to you? You have several bastards who can inherit and carry on the line. As does mother."* That last was meant to hurt Father, and it had worked. End of argument.

His father had never brought the subject up again, but Alastair still worried over that night, the angry shouts and possible retaliation.

He shook away the memory, and with the onerous task of confronting his friend finished, he went to talk to Morgan. He wanted a chance to raise the boy's hackles again. Something about him. He was smart, earnest, and prickly, and that combination was a challenge. He wanted that fine body tense with pleasure above him and wanted to match wits with the boy, but Morgan made excuses to leave each time he tried to start a conversation. With Lydia in the midst of her class, Morgan was trapped.

Leaning with his head tilted to the sun, Morgan had a faint sheen of sweat on his strong neck. Alastair wanted to lick the freshly shaven skin and chase the salty moisture up to those perfect lips. Forcing down his lust, he said, "You and Miss Lydia seem to be benefiting from our hospitality."

Morgan looked his way, then closed his eyes again. The man never jumped or startled. Must have nerves of steel.

"The weather is quite nice, and the air is breathable. Since Lydia has improved so rapidly, she now believes me when I tell her the ailment is not consumption. You cannot imagine how happy that makes me. One of the many doctors I dragged her to diagnosed it as a consumptive illness, and we believed him." The boy continued more rapidly, as if fighting off the need to weep. "Anyone would benefit from leaving London. It has always been our home, but I never realized what a dreadful place it is."

"I agree. My mother still lives there; even though she can afford to live anywhere, she has no desire to leave. Can't understand it myself."

At the mention of some personal history, Morgan turned his full gaze his way. *Oh, so he is curious about me? Good. Good indeed.*

He nodded at the man's sister. "She seems much improved."

"Yes, thank the heavens. I worried she wouldn't survive until we sailed." Morgan glanced sheepishly his way. "One of the reasons the delay irritated me a bit."

He snorted. "A bit? I thought you hoped to rip my head off, which would have done no good at all, as there would have been no captain for your trip."

Morgan laughed, a deep, full sound, and Alastair could not drag his eyes away from the man's face, a breathtaking image when he smiled. He'd been wrong in the tavern. This man personified beautiful. His nose and frowns were irresistible, but when he smiled, it changed his looks from handsome to utterly magnificent.

"I must admit, my temper is my greatest flaw. Please forgive me. It is just…" He cast a glance at his sister. "She is my only family. It is my responsibility to keep her safe."

Anger, protectiveness, and happiness. This man had a zest for life. He could not stop staring at Morgan. Hell, half his seamen were tripping over themselves to get a look at this man. Daylight highlighting his features, the breeze in his hair, he looked like a fae being who commanded the weather.

Morgan noticed his regard. He glanced over, licked his lips slowly, then smiled.

Of course Alastair's gaze followed the action, and he was certain Morgan sensed his full-blown lust.

To give himself time to settle his arousal, he turned and pointed at the impromptu classroom. "Your sister is an amazing young lady. So accepting of differences." There were at least three different races in her class, and one woman, Tim, who looked more like a lad in her shapeless sailor's slops. She'd been a street urchin who changed her name and took to wearing boys' clothes around ten years of age to keep from being pimped out. She was tough, handy with a blade, and held her own with the crew and her duties; most of the time the men forgot she was a woman until someone new hired on. Miss Lydia treated all of them with respect and did not talk down to anyone for not knowing their letters.

"My sister is a precious thing. Sometimes I wonder if she weren't sent directly from heaven to show us all what humanity is. Then I wonder why God would have sent her to me." He smirked.

"Perhaps to show you there is some gray in your black-and-white world?"

There was a slight bristling before Morgan relaxed again. "Perhaps."

"I've told my crew that she is to be treated with the utmost respect. They will look after her; they are a good lot. You can relax your vigil."

The boy seemed to inwardly melt at that comment. "I've watched after her since our father died, and then she got sick a few years ago. I didn't know what to do, how to make her well. You cannot believe what a relief—" He broke off, his voice thick. "She is talking about the future again. She'd stopped doing that for such a long time."

"Your mother?"

"Died in childbed when much too young."

He placed a hand on the boy's granite-firm arm. He could feel the muscles flex even through a lawn shirt and smoothly worn wool coat. What did this man do to develop muscles upon muscles? "You have done a good job. She has survived, you are taking her away from god-awful London Town, and she has obviously thrived under your guardianship. Take some time to enjoy your first-rate work, to let yourself enjoy being free from obligations and worry. She is in a safe place. Take the chance to be young and alive again."

The look Morgan gave him could have singed hair. "I might... I just might do that, Captain Breckenridge."

Oh, the way that gaze and those words sent his world spinning on its axis. Time to set the stage for a more intimate encounter. "I have adjusted our contract to accommodate the alteration in our estimated arrival to Dominica and to verify the amount of cargo loaded. Come by after supper, and I will give you your copy."

"I'll come by after I watch the sunset. Have you noticed how fast the transition is from light to complete darkness on the water?"

Fighting a smile, Alastair said, "Yes, I have noticed. See you after supper, then?"

Nodding slightly, Morgan stared at his lips.

It was nearly the hardest thing he'd ever done, leaving that spot at that time and pretending he had something important to do.

* * * *

"Here is your copy of the document." Alastair enjoyed how good Morgan looked sitting across the desk from him, lantern light bouncing off the low open-beamed ceiling, turning his hair almost auburn. Broad shoulders dressed in slightly worn, dark-brown wool filled the captain's cabin, making the room look less lonely than it had in a long while. He held out the tightly rolled parchment they signed moments earlier, and leaned over the table. "I am glad you agreed with the new conditions of our contract."

Morgan reached for the contract without rising from his chair. "They were minor alterations, nothing for me to dispute."

A bit of the devil got into Alastair, and he pulled the document just out of reach. Morgan reached farther, and again he retreated. With his head ever so slightly tilted, Morgan lowered his arm and regarded Alastair.

Having obviously decided, the man rose, moved around the table, took two steps closer, and then one more unneeded step before bending down. He was so close, Alastair could count the flecks of gold in his eyes.

"Why the game of keep away?" Smooth as river-washed stone and warm as the first sip of good rum, the words glided across Alastair's skin.

Morgan reached for the paper slowly, giving Alastair time to yank it away if he desired. Oh, he desired, but not for a game of keep away. He held still until a large, warm hand curled over his fingers. Closing his eyes, he made an audible swallow.

"Not pulling away now?"

Stupidly, he shook his head. For the life of Neptune, he could not think of anything to say. Too much concentration focused on the erotic tingles filling his belly.

Opening his eyes, he saw Morgan lean closer. So close, he heard slow, steady breathing. Close enough to catch the hint of eau de cologne. Close enough to see a flare of nostrils, the enlarging pupils. Damn. Morgan was aroused, highly aroused.

Desire flooded his veins, complete with shortness of breath and a painful constriction in too tight trousers.

Those looks that lasted a second too long now made sense, but not the looks of regret, not the clenched teeth and clenched fists, the ridiculous anger. Alastair made it clear he was interested, available. Why hadn't the boy simply accepted the offer, which he obviously wanted, instead of letting frustration build?

Time to relieve the boy's frustration; time to take what he had longed for since that foggy afternoon in London. He touched Morgan's cheek, rubbing a finger slowly down rough, half-day stubble. For a moment Morgan paused, jaw tightened, seemed to rethink his actions, then dipped his head.

Unable to breathe, he closed eyes and waited for the kiss he longed for since the Red Pig. The whisper of breath caressed his lips. So close now. Anticipation sent him forward. And then, just like that, Morgan took the scroll from Alastair's limp, numb fingers and slipped from the bunk into the dark, cold, lonely North Atlantic night.

DAMNATION, WHAT HAD he just done? Rhain chastised himself as he stormed down to his cabin to stow the document.

He'd promised himself he would not—*not*—do this again with any man after Robert. Except for a few lapses that led him to visit a molly house or two…or perhaps three…he'd kept that promise.

And now I go and almost sit in the pirate's lap. Almost kissed that irreverent mouth, for God's sake. What the bloody hell was wrong with him?

He could be content with a woman, have a wife, a family. Couldn't he? Perhaps meet her in Dominica.

He found women attractive after all, had been with a few, even though he preferred men. Plus, being with a woman would have an added benefit. He would be able to distance himself from her enough so as to never again suffer a broken heart.

Robert had nearly crippled him with an unanticipated rejection. He would not go through that pain again. And this pirate… He was quick-witted, intriguing, tough but kind. Compassionate at times. He had the power to snare and crush an unsuspecting heart.

Add the power of the captain's allure to this damn ship, which felt like a safe haven, like he could do anything and not be caught, or if caught, receive a salacious wink and nothing more, and that led to problems. The feeling of safety could trick and then trap and smash an already bruised heart.

What a stupid fool, he. With his uncommon lusts, he would never be safe. From now on, he would keep his guard up, avoid the pirate, and keep his damn kisses to himself.

Chapter Four

Casablanca, Morocco

It was obvious they were far from England before ropes even touched the decrepit dock. Rhain worried it would not hold up under the added weight of the *Hurricane*'s men and cargo.

Trees of a shape he'd never seen before Lisbon stood sentinel to round-capped buildings. Sounds were different. Exotic music filled the air. The predominant language held a melodious flair, loud and incomprehensible. Rhain reveled in the discordant music played on drums, cymbals, and wind instruments.

Lydia squeezed his arm and bounced on her little feet.

Rhain laughed. "Lydia, you aren't excited, are you?"

"Of course I am excited. This is the most spectacular adventure we have ever experienced. Probably will ever have. Look at all the colorful clothes." She took a deep breath and closed vivid blue eyes. "Just smell the air."

The air smelled like a bubbling pot of the Indian curry favored by one of his father's friends who'd spent time in India and brought back a cook. He suspected the cook also served as convenient lover, but that was purely supposition.

He breathed in the warm, fragrant air. Spicy indeed. His stomach rumbled, and Lydia laughed.

"Did you ever realize life could be this wonderful?"

He patted her hand, surprised he no longer held anger at this, their second delay on the voyage to the plantation.

Lisbon had been a disappointment. The *Hurricane* had slipped in to dock while he and Lydia slept. They were not allowed to leave the ship. They were in port only eight hours, off-loading some valuable cargo under the colonial flag.

Since France expanded its occupation into Portugal, it was no longer safe to fly a British flag. It was best to off-load, reload, and sail before officials could inspect papers.

Portugal was sunny and full of life. All the buildings were white with terra-cotta roofs, and a distant sandstone castle sat on a hill surrounded by those unusual umbrella-shaped trees.

Lydia had wished to explore Lisbon, but Casablanca seemed to make up for her disappointment.

The city radiated an exotic allure. He found himself impatient to disembark, explore, and take it all in.

One hour later they shared an open, rattling wagon with the no-nonsense First Mate Dunn and six armed seamen. The first mate was a small man with unruly mud-brown hair, but he held himself with the arrogance of someone who knew how to survive. Rhain was convinced that Lydia would be safe on this outing, given their escorts.

The small city was flat and sandy and frenzied from one end to the other. Unlike London, there didn't seem to be any quiet streets.

Lydia purchased lush silks, and he bought sweet, fragrant spices, envisioning their cook in Dominica making sweets and exquisite dishes of exemplary taste.

The streets were crowded. Most city inhabitants wore loose voluminous dress, very unlike the dock laborers, who worked in very little clothing.

He tried in vain to avoid staring at one young man loitering in a doorway. His lean, supple chest was bare. His long, straight, black hair reminded him of their captain. The mahogany skin did not.

The youth held his gaze and sauntered to the wagon, then walked briskly beside them, stroking Rhain's hand, uttering incomprehensible words. However, the black eyes promised something Rhain understood and knew quite well.

Lydia jerked back and gasped as the seamen jeered and encouraged the boy, one being so bold as to squeeze the lad's arse.

Rhain knew if he were alone, he would be very tempted to accept this invitation; instead, he shook his head, tossed the whore a coin, and urged the driver forward.

Oddly, as they rumbled through the city, the youth's attentions spurred immodest fantasies of one pirate captain instead of the young Casablancan prostitute.

* * * *

That night, enjoying a light meal of spicy meat and fruit pie, Rhain watched Lydia unfold, refold, and repack her new silk. One piece of silk caught his attention. It was a shimmery dark emerald. Lydia held it against her body and danced in place. "Won't this make a lovely ball gown, Rhain?"

He nodded. His sister was always lovely to him, but that extraordinary color and the lay of the fabric made her look like a queen.

"You will break many hearts if you have that cloth sewn into a gown."

She laughed, held the silk up to his chest, and assessed him, her head tilting to one side, then the other. "You know… If we made this into a waistcoat, it would drive your pirate to distraction."

"Lydia! I've asked you not to discuss—"

"Oh, come now, you have seen how he looks at you."

Actually he hadn't, but it was a sure bet he would dream about green silk and desirable pirates this night.

* * * *

"You are mad, sir." Dunn's tone was possibly more irritated than Alastair had heard in a long time.

"It's the dry season; no reason to stop at the Canaries, anyway."

"But it will be two weeks more before we can reprovision."

"If we don't stop, we will gain time."

"It will make a difference of two days at the most."

Alastair sighed. He did not like taking such a long stretch knowing there would be no place to stop for fresh water.

"What if we hit the doldrums? What then?"

He rubbed the bridge of his nose. "Dunn. Do you remember what happened the last time we stopped for water during the dry season?"

Dunn turned his back and crossed his arms.

"Yes, I see you do remember. We were almost stoned for trying to extract water from a damn mud hole. I do not plan to repeat that experience."

"It was five years ago. Our first year sailing together." Dunn relaxed and looked at Alastair once more.

"Yes, it was. Now, if you look here on the map"—he pointed to a route they had never tried before and continued—"you can see there is a third route marked. It goes straight down, without stopping at the Canaries. It is more direct, so it might save us a week if we don't stop at those blasted dry islands."

"It is riskier because we are already several days from our last stop."

"By God, Dunn. We will make up time." He thumped his hand on the table, and his quill fell from its holder. He said more quietly, "That is time we need."

When Dunn still did not look convinced, he said, "Damn it, Dunn, I'm willing to chance it."

"I will set a course as per your orders, but I want the ship's log-book to say I am not in agreement."

"Agreed. Now go alter our heading before we run aground on the cursed islands."

Dunn left, and Alastair had time to worry that he might have made a very bad decision.

* * * *

Rhain stood on one foot, slipping his other into trousers. There was an annoyingly loud whistle before the ship tilted to one side and turned toward his right, throwing him off balance and into the wall. If not for the tiny dimensions of the room, he would have fallen to the wood-planked floor.

There were shouts and the sound of feet pounding overhead. "What the bloody hell is going on?"

Lydia knocked on his door as he finished pulling up and then fastening his trousers. "Rhain, what the devil is happening?"

"Lydia, back in your room, and lock the door until I determine what the problem is." He grabbed a shirt and opened his door. "And do stop swearing. I believe the seamen are a bad influence on you."

She stood there, hands on hips, feet spread apart to keep her balance like an old sailor, her curls a frizzy halo around her head. "You can't expect me to wait down here until you come and call me forth."

He pointed at her door. "In! And stay there until I come for you."

She glared at him until the door closed and he could no longer see her expression.

He flung on the shirt, not bothering to tie the laces. Bouncing off one wall then the other as the ship changed direction and speed, he stumbled to the stairs.

Flinging open the topside door, he was momentarily blinded by the sun shining directly in his eyes from a cloudless morning sky. After blinking several times, he made out sailors running this way and that, pulling, yanking, and hauling things. They resembled oversize ants running back and forth to defend their hill.

Very unusual that most of them were smiling.

Shouts filled the air, and nobody paid him the slightest bit of attention. Not even when he tried to ask a few bare-chested men in wide-legged breeches the ship's status. Then he found the captain standing tall and imposing at the helm, shouting orders and laughing. Amid the chaos, the captain of the ship threw his head back and roared his mirth. The pirate was completely mad.

Rhain struggled his way to the helm, stepping around scurrying men with ropes.

The captain looked his direction, looked away, and then snapped his attention immediately to Rhain. The humor left his face. He pointed and shouted, "Belowdeck. Now."

Rhain shook his head and took the last ten steps to where the captain scowled at him.

"Belowdeck; it is not safe up here for you."

"What the bloody hell are you doing?" He looked behind him but saw no privateer running up their back side.

Breckenridge pointed forward to a ship so far away, it looked like a toy on a very large pond. "We are going to seize that ship."

"Whatever for?"

The devilish grin Breckenridge spared him froze his breath. No, God no. Were they going to board that ship? Would there be a fight? What of Lydia? "What will you do if you catch that boat?"

"First of all, that is a *ship*, not a boat. And if we *catch* her, we will board her and take no prisoners."

"A fight? Sir, you are a pirate. A real swashbuckling, sailor-killing pirate?" He clutched the captain's arm, gripping with his full strength.

Breckenridge winced.

"You cannot do this; what of Lydia?"

"Is safe down below where you need to be." He shook off Rhain's grip and pointed to a very large, bald seaman. "Take him belowdeck now." He pointed at Rhain. "And stay there until this is done to make certain he and Miss Lydia stay put."

The sailor said, "Aye, sir," and grabbed Rhain's arm, half pulling him to the belowdeck hatchway.

As if the morning couldn't grow any worse, there stood Lydia, holding on to the hatchway frame, big eyes taking in every sight, a slight smile on her lips, but with eyebrows pinched.

He pulled his arm from the sailor and said, "Down."

Lydia flew down the stairs and into her room.

Rhain followed her in and locked the door.

"What is it? What's going on?"

He answered while scouring the small room for a weapon, any weapon.

No matter what, he would not let Lydia suffer at the hands of a marauding band of sailors if the other ship was unfortunately the victor.

"Stop disordering my room; what do you want?"

"A weapon." He'd left his dagger in his locked trunk. If there was nothing in here, he would move Lydia to his room and dig out the small dagger he usually wore on his person.

"Let me." She sighed and dug into her portmanteau, pulling out a wicked-looking knife, which she handed to him, handle first.

"Where the devil?"

"I purchased it when you told me we were going to Dominica. Wanted to be prepared for wild animals or vile bandits." She grinned.

He sat down on her bunk. Was the whole world insane? His six-and-a-half-stone sister purchased a very large knife—not a dagger which would be much more useful in a fight, but a knife—and was excited about fending off wild beasts, and their captain was getting ready to start a battle in the middle of the damn Atlantic.

Listening to the shouts and footfalls overhead, he took a deep breath and rubbed his face with one hand, the other clenching the knife.

Lydia sat on the bunk next to him. "Are you sure it's not safe to watch? At least until we reach the other ship?"

He growled.

* * * *

It seemed like years as they sat in that cramped room, listening to men shouting and feet running overhead, but it was probably only an hour or two. Rhain noticed the decreased speed as a rap came on Lydia's door.

"Well, then, looks like it is safe to leave your berth now," said a muffled voice through the thin wood.

Rhain vibrated with rage.

Lydia touched his arm. "Rhain? The knife." She held out a hand that seemed too small to even hold the bulky thing.

He handed it over and then went in search of the pirate captaining this damn vessel.

Obviously, the captain had authorized tapping a cask of liquor, for the crew were all singing some bawdy sea tunes and upending tin cups.

"Bloody damn wonderful." Just what they needed—a drunken crew while another pirate ship lurked around after dark with a bull's-eye trained on the *Hurricane*. It took him several moments to find the captain. The man sat on deck in the shade, quietly talking with First Mate Dunn. They were both smiling and, fortunately, not drinking.

They stopped smiling as he neared.

"A word with you, Captain." The title was little more than a sneer as it left his tight lips.

Breckenridge nodded and whispered something to his first mate, who stared at Rhain with barely disguised suspicion.

ALASTAIR STEPPED ONE foot over the threshold to his cabin when he was launched against the mahogany-paneled bulkhead, and a large slab of muscle pressed him painfully against the raised wainscoting. He winced at the pain on his bruised tailbone.

Hot, fresh breath caressed his cheek as Morgan spat out all the egregious things that ever happened in the world and how it was his opinion that they were all Captain Breckenridge's fault. "...on top of everything, you are allowing your crew to inebriate on rum."

"Whew, but you have a foul tongue when your bile is up. And for the record, they are drinking grog, not rum." Despite the interesting dialogue, he didn't quite follow the full bombast because of the distracting bulge smashed up against his hip bone, which made his own rod swell and lengthen.

"Additionally, how dare you jeopardize the health and safety of my sister, a woman under your protection, sir, with your attempt at piracy?" He shook Alastair's shoulders for effect.

Damn, but he was spectacular in his fury. Morgan's unlaced, loose shirt showed a firm, pale chest with a nest of crisp, dark hair. Alastair couldn't even speak, for his breath came too fast and his heart pounded.

Morgan leaned in closer, and his lips almost brushed his cheek when he whispered in Alastair's ear. "What do you have to say for yourself, you hypocritical arse?"

Alastair loved being overpowered, but there were few men of his acquaintance who could do it. He leaned his head against the bulkhead and arched into the furious body holding him captive.

Morgan must have thought it was a play to escape and leaned more weight against him.

Alastair closed his eyes and leaned his head back. "Yes." The word escaped his lips before his brain engaged, and the heady weight left him with the speed of a nor'easter.

Bereft of the sensual weight, he slowly opened his eyes and tried to control his breathing.

In the middle of the room, Morgan rubbed his hands over his face, his shoulders hunched.

What a fool thing to have taken on passengers. He knew better. But damn, from the moment he'd seen this large, strong man, he'd wanted him. He still wanted him, even though the man held more anger in him than a bucketful of hot vipers.

He walked over and poured them both a measure of brandy. "Here."

Morgan took the offered glass and downed it with a wince.

Tracing the sharp-edged crystal patterns under his fingers, he said, "You knew there were dangers when you signed on to travel this time of year. You booked the passage anyway."

"I did not expect my captain to go out of his way to look for trouble." The words were low and rumbled as if each one was a profanity.

"You and your sister were never in danger. Giving chase does wonders for the crew's disposition. Gets everyone's blood up so they stay sharp and pay attention."

"That is the most ridiculous... And what if you'd caught that other ship, what then? How could you have ensured Lydia's safety if this boat was boarded?"

"That would not have occurred. And by the way, this is also a ship, not a boat. A one-hundred-man brigantine, to be precise, although we don't run at full capacity."

Morgan huffed and tossed one hand toward the heavens. "You perhaps have too much faith in your motley crew, *my captain*. For I assure you, the other *boat* would have a crew too, and they would be defending themselves with great passion against pirates."

He turned his back so Morgan couldn't see his humor, for he fully suspected this proud boy would turn violent if his anger were mocked. He wasn't mocking, though; actually, he liked that Morgan thought him piratical, that he thought his crew intimidating, that he called him *my captain*. Fact was, he really liked this prickly boy. He was a bit single-minded in his devotion to his sister perhaps, but who could fault anyone for that? Alastair barely knew his stepsisters, probably would not recognize them if he met them on the street. So he admired the siblings' devotion to each other.

With his misplaced humor under control, he turned to confront Morgan. "I have methods of protecting my ship, and no one, *no one*, has the authority to question my methods. I will tell you a secret, but it is between you…" He stalked slowly toward Morgan. "…and me. You will tell no one under threat of death. Understand?"

Morgan swallowed and took a couple of steps back until his thighs encountered the heavy oak table.

THE SWITCH IN power happened so fast, Rhain had no time to wrest back control. Now he stood trapped, with the table behind him, and the captain mere inches away, his expression cold and polite. No, that wasn't quite accurate. The expression could be called chilling.

He'd known this man could be dangerous, but he'd also seen compassion, so he did not realize just how ruthless this pirate captain could be.

Breckenridge moved in slowly and said in a whisper, "That was a French ship whose captain thinks little of taking what he wants from Americans and English. They attacked us last year. Stole some cargo and killed eight of my men. We chased them today to put the fear of fifty good men with swords and five new cannons into their yellow-livered souls. They will not attack us again. Of that you can be certain."

He swallowed. "So you never intended to catch them?"

"I steered this ship, and she can run on the wind; the other cannot. If I'd wished to catch them, they would be paying their respects to Davy Jones as we speak. Your sister is safer currently than before my display." With lightning-quick reflexes, Breckenridge pushed him back until he lay on the hard surface of the table. The athletic man climbed up, the table groaning with their combined weight, until he straddled Rhain's crotch. He leaned down and brushed a light, warm kiss to his lips. And oh, God, the sensation of that light touch sang through his entire being. He no longer felt the hard table under his back, couldn't feel the contact at their groin, only that soft kiss.

He reached up to touch that perfect face, but Breckenridge pinned his wrists against his sides and slid sweet kisses down his cheek, over his jaw, and along his neck. He was certain he could overpower the man, but he found he lacked the desire to do so. He lifted his hips, pressing their crotches closer together.

The captain arched up, closed his eyes, and hissed. Light streamed in through the windows and lit the captain's face.

Rhain took a moment to devour the beauty. Dark lashes so long it looked like the man used kohl, but he did not. A straight, thin nose and firm, dark lips. The gold ring in his ear flashed in the light. Lovely.

"I'm sorry for my outburst. I didn't know your plans."

"Obviously." The one word sounded as if it were squeezed from an overtight sausage casing.

"If you had but told me."

Taking a shuddering breath, the captain said, "I am not in the habit of divulging my strategy. And now, if you'll excuse me." He sprang from the table and started looking through drawers. "I have a celebration to attend with my men. See yourself out."

The cold dismissal delivered the same effect as a winter dunking in the Thames. He sat up slowly, hating the loss of the captain's heat, his touch.

He adjusted his clothing and left to find Lydia. Seemed he had more apologies yet to give today.

As he opened the door, Breckenridge said over his shoulder, "And, Mr. Morgan, I expect you and your sister to dine with me tonight in my cabin. Arrive at sundown unless you want cold rations."

Chapter Five

It was a joy to watch Miss Lydia in a shimmering blue dinner gown and Dunn in his olive-green uniform interact. They acted as if they'd been friends since birth. Surprising, since she was gently bred and Dunn fought his way up every step of the way to attain his current position.

Watching Morgan was a different story altogether. Just admiring the man forced him to fight lust one minute and then fight annoyance at the man's aloofness the next. Why wouldn't he relax, let down his guard, enjoy himself? It was obvious he wanted to.

Alastair truly believed they could interact as well or even better than Miss Lydia and Dunn. If only the man would stop looking at him through his preconceived biases. Shattering biases was the point of tonight.

He topped off Morgan's wineglass.

Alastair wore his nicest dinner clothes and brought out his drawing room manners. He rarely played dress-up on ship and rarely when in the colonies. His mother, however, dragged him all over London when he was in town. Showing off her beautiful son, she liked to say.

Slightly disgusted that he'd dressed up like a peacock to impress a man he liked an ounce too much, he watched the man in question.

Morgan sat quietly in the brown suit he wore the first time Alastair met him. The man observed everything—the crystal glasses, the silver cutlery, his sister, Dunn. Everything, that was, except the peacock in the finery.

Pushing his braid behind his ear, he tried to look less like a fop and more like the successful sea captain he'd become.

Miss Lydia and his first mate carried the conversation for several minutes while everyone enjoyed the chicken, biscuits, pea mash, and Madeira wine.

The fowl was a rare treat this far into a sail, but Cook usually kept a few alive for a special dinner, such as tonight. The bird, although tough, combined well with the wine and onion sauce, making the dishes savory on his tongue and very welcome.

When dessert of poached apples in brandy was served, Alastair decided it was time to draw the handsome, quiet guest into conversation. "My dear Mr. Morgan?"

The man's head swiveled toward him so fast, his hair fell over his forehead. Straightening his locks, he cleared his voice and said, "Yes?"

"I am pleased you and Miss Lydia have shown no signs of seasickness. Have you suffered from any digestive distress?"

The young man smiled, showing just a hint of strong white teeth. "Happily, no. It seems the sea agrees with both Lydia and myself. I rather think if plantation running doesn't agree with me, I shall petition a position as yardman on your ship."

They all laughed, but the thought of having that man under his command was intoxicating. "Mate Dunn, is there room for Mr. Morgan on crew?"

Dunn pursed his lips and tapped them with an index finger. "Now that I think about it, we do have a need for an undercook."

Morgan replied with a look of mock disgust.

Good to know he could enjoy teasing directed his way. Perhaps the wine diluted prickles.

Alastair once again poured more wine into the young man's wineglass while his attention was on discussing his plantation. The way his face lit and his body animated, one could tell that he was looking forward to the challenge of getting the little plot of land running efficiently and profitably.

"Our plantation is not an established one. My father purchased it shortly before he died, and the overseer is slowly making improvements. The first four years, a neighbor leased the land to raise goats; then I asked the overseer to handle the planting by hiring help. We've seen no profit this past two years. Well, truth be told, we've not seen any profit yet." He shrugged and took a sip of wine.

"Higher taxes and reinvestment in the property, you see. Lydia helped me form a plan for increasing profits. So I fully expect that after I negotiate a lower tax rate and utilize the changes I have read about, we shall start seeing a profit. After all, sugar prices have never been as high as they are currently. It is only a matter of time before we are sitting on a little gold mine."

Miss Lydia beamed at her older brother. "Rhain has researched this very, very fully. He is incredibly smart for a man of only four and twenty."

"Did you go to university, then, Mr. Morgan?" Dunn fortunately asked, so he did not have to. He found he was much too interested in this passenger.

Morgan was in the middle of a large swallow, so his sister chimed in on what must be a favored topic. "Rhain had a short but adequate education. He was the absolute best at fencing and pugilism in school. He is smart, strong, and agile, so if anyone can make the right decisions about profits, it will be he."

"Lydia." The large man blushed under her praise, and with flushed cheeks, he appeared younger than twenty.

How unexpectedly endearing.

Alastair could envision the man playing sports. He was strong and muscular with a domineering personality; of course he would be good at everything. Alastair would bet he was an expert in bed sports as well. He topped off the wineglass again.

"Actually, Lydia is a wizard with numbers. She keeps my accounts and is always finding ways to economize and notices when a tradesman is trying to overcharge." Morgan sported a contented glow and was positively nice and, well, almost sweet-natured at the moment. With that relaxed smile, he looked delectable.

"Miss Lydia, I must say I have always detested keeping the books, and I put that task off until I absolutely must do it."

"Truly, sir. I would be happy to catch them up for you, if you wish. It would give me something to do that I enjoy."

He didn't need to even think about her offer before accepting. If anyone offered to order his books, he was willing to let them try. He had not even wanted to look at them after Morocco. Too damn disheartening to see his plan to build his own fleet slip further and further out of his grasp. They made plans to start her working on the accounts ledgers the next day.

"These partially settled islands can be unstable at times; do you feel safe going alone, just the two of you?" Dunn asked.

"Hmm. I don't think I need to worry. After all, Lydia owns a very wicked-looking knife." When the laughter died down, he continued, "In addition, my foreman informed me that the new investments have made the place quite comfortable to live in."

"I must say, I was pleased to hear so after Rhain told me we were moving there. I'm afraid I like a certain amount of comforts."

"We all do, my dear girl." Dunn patted her hand, and she briefly grasped his fingers.

"The currency on many of these islands is unstable, and there can be excessive lawlessness. I cannot say much about Dominica as I have never been there; have you, Dunn?"

"No, actually the closest I've been is Barbados, where we will stop on the way. Now, what a paradise that island is. I'm certain Dominica, being so close to Barbados, must be just as grand."

"Is that so? Do tell us."

Dunn regaled Miss Lydia with tales of mountains, waterfalls, birds of astonishing plumage, and game so abundant one did not need to raise animals for food.

During the narrative, he noticed Morgan looking at him. When he glanced back, the boy would drop his gaze to the table.

They all ate heartily, this being a treat five days after leaving Casablanca. With the food consumed, port was savored, and everyone complained of eating too much.

Dunn began his leave-taking, claiming an early morning of duties.

There were the expected "thank yous" and "lovely evenings," and the guests started filing out.

"Mr. Morgan, a moment if you please," he said.

The boy looked over his shoulder. "I should walk Lydia to her berth."

"I'm certain Mate Dunn won't mind seeing she arrives there safely."

Dunn lit up like a full moon on a cloudless South Pacific sea. "Not at all. My lady?" He held out his arm.

Miss Lydia took it, giggling. "Oh, how gallant, sir. I am quite pleased to have your protection."

"Lydia?"

"I'll be fine, Rhain. Enjoy your evening." The saucy girl fluttered her lashes at him.

She was a rare one, for a certainty, but Alastair wasn't at all convinced this experience would be good for her future comportment.

Morgan stepped back into the room, and Alastair closed and locked the door.

"You wished a word with me, then?" He cocked his brow, looking somehow small in his big body.

"No, actually. I wanted to do this." He slammed that big body face-first against the door, yanked down his coat so that his arms were trapped, and licked the side of his face. The faint smell of eau de cologne went perfectly with the lemony-sweet taste of his skin. His cock went poker-hard before he could even swear. "God. For such a prickly bastard, you taste so damn sweet."

BECAUSE OF HIS wine-muddled head, it took Rhain a moment to realize what happened. He first thought Breckenridge planned to physically harm him, but then, with a tongue against his neck and the grind of a very hard erection against his hip, he realized the attack was for pleasure instead.

The slide of that warm tongue along his cheek tickled. He would have chuckled if not for his rigid cock pressed against the hard surface of the door. He moaned. There was no way to stop the sound from escaping his throat even if he wanted to.

"Ah, yes. You want me too." Breckenridge rubbed against him. "I thought as much."

Want him? Rhain had been wood-hard all evening. Needed him was a better description.

"Turn around, then."

He struggled to remove his coat, which currently acted like manacles. "No."

He was again pushed against the wood.

"Don't remove your constraint, or I will tie you to the table. I have plans for you, and that requires you being unable to touch me. Understand?"

Rhain nodded, staring over the pirate's shoulder at the single row of large windows, one tied open, allowing in a cool breeze and the sound of waves lapping against wood.

"Is that acceptable to you?"

He thought for a moment and then nodded again.

"Good."

Without another word, he was spun around and shoved against the door for the third time. This time, his arms were trapped behind him, and Breckenridge had an evil—no, not evil—wickedly playful grin and half-closed eyes.

"Don't move, or I *will* tie you up. Now behave."

The man's silky tenor mentioning bindings nearly undid Rhain. Again all he could do was nod. And he kept nodding as the captain slipped to his knees, unfastening Rhain's falls as he went.

Looking up, not breaking their gaze, Breckenridge slowly pulled the falls out of his way and untied drawers, dragging cool fingers across heated skin as he did so.

His aching prick loomed only inches away from wet, perfect lips.

The captain looked down and finished pulling the cloth away until Rhain's prick sprang out. "Oh, bloody hell. If that is not the most perfect cock I've ever seen." He licked from the base to the tip. "Even here you taste like a salty dessert."

Good God! He was going to come. The slide of that warm tongue, his—what was it now, four months?—abstinence, and the alcohol, were altogether too much. He groaned and started to launch over into ecstasy.

"Oh no, not yet." Breckenridge grabbed the base of his cock and squeezed. The pressure in his balls became bearable, but just barely.

"It…it's been a while for me."

"Aye, I can see that. Not to worry. If you blow, then we will start all over. Ready to commence?"

"God, yes! Suck me."

"With pleasure." Breckenridge clasped those beautiful lips onto his prick without releasing the clamp on the base. That bit of discomfort was enough to keep him from coming and allowed him to enjoy the surge of pleasure as the smooth male mouth slipped slowly up and down his shaft. The man hummed as he sank deep, and the vibration turned him nearly comatose with pleasure.

So close. So why did he stop the pirate at that critical juncture with a no and snapped open his eyes?

His pirate stopped immediately and sat on his haunches, staring at him.

"Good God, what are you waiting for? Come up here."

At Rhain's command, Breckenridge stood and in a fraction of a moment was so close, Rhain could feel heat radiating from the man.

"Help me off with this damn coat so I can touch you." His coat was whipped off so fast, his wrists burned. Once free, he used unbound hands to undo the thick maroon belt hidden under the pirate's dinner jacket. It came open with a smoothness of long use, and dark red showed under the buckle. He almost laughed at the idea of anyone wearing a belt that color, but then realized the pirate would look good draped in such a vibrant shade.

Belt out of the way, he opened his pirate's trousers and extracted a gorgeous, long, thick cock.

"I want this," he said as he reached and grasped the iron-hard length covered in smooth, silky skin.

Whimpering, Breckenridge grabbed his hand.

Watching his large, masculine hand wrapped around that pretty cock was akin to looking at a masterpiece. Perfect, precious, and worthy of admiration. After several slow strokes of the pirate's cock, he glanced at the man's handsome face. He looked right at Rhain, eyes half shuttered, head tilted back, lips moist and parted.

God, but he wanted to kiss that mouth. Truth be told, he'd desired to kiss this pirate from the first time he'd seen him lounging against the door at the Red Pig. And so he did just that.

Lowering his lips to his pirate's, he watched the man's eyes flutter shut. The light caress of these particular lips consumed all his senses. He no longer heard the noise of the ship or felt the sway of the boards under his feet. No longer smelled the leftover food. Closing his eyes, he reveled in the sensation of the kiss. His lips tingled, his ears buzzed, and his body hummed.

He could be content here for hours, but his pirate deepened the kiss, grabbed the back of his head, ground their lips together, then slipped in a tongue that tasted like apples and cinnamon.

The kiss was wet and loud; the sound of breathing, sucking, and licking entered his ears and raced down to tease his rod. A surge of lust like he'd never felt before took over. He spun them around and pressed Breckenridge against the door, slamming their cocks together.

He gripped both hard rods in one fist and started rocking.

Wrapping his arms around Rhain's shoulders, Breckenridge leaned forward and sealed their lips more tightly together, and they kissed while Rhain stroked and rocked. The grip and glide of smooth skin over that long hard cock shot waves of pleasure through his overly aroused body. He was primed again and ready to blow, but he would not come until his pirate did. The man, so beautiful at all times, would be spectacular in the throes of passion.

Breaking the kiss, he leaned back and sped up his stroking. "Come for me, Captain. I want to know if you cry out or are silent when you spend."

Mouth open, breaths coming in rapid gasps, Breckenridge leaned his head against the wood, closed his eyes, and moaned, the sound erotic and corporeal. It would be a challenge to hold off long enough to watch his pirate's climax.

It took no longer than a minute before his pirate writhed against him, head rocking from side to side, husky whimpers slipping from his lips. And then he came, the man's whole body tensing as streams of hot semen covered Rhain's hand and both their pricks. And just as he'd fantasized, Breckenridge was spectacular in his passion.

The combination of slick spend and hard cock against his own proved more than he could handle and launched him into that space that only another man could send him. A euphoric place of lust, passion, and danger. But this time, there was that and something more. Something that almost felt like sugar pumped directly into his veins. He shivered and embraced the transportation into bliss.

* * * *

When the after-climax haze wore off, Rhain let Breckenridge go and collapsed into a chair, not bothering to do up his clothes.

"By God, that was magnificent," Breckenridge whispered as he stumbled to his own chair. Then, with long limbs and lyrical movements, he poured two large glasses of port.

Breckenridge was so very graceful that occasionally he moved in such a way as to appear feline, or perhaps even feminine, but then he would move again and be all masculine beauty. Somehow the man was a perfect combination of both sexes. All through dinner, Rhain couldn't help but watch the man who looked sensual as hell whether in his current black, white, and green formal wear or in his disreputable ship attire. He would gently brush that flirty braid over one shoulder, toy with the stem of his wineglass, and tilt his head to listen to Lydia or First Mate Dunn. He didn't tilt his head when he listened to Rhain, though. No, then his gaze was direct, hungry, head held in a dominant, forthright manner. Like a predator assessing another dangerous beast.

The fascination he held for this man drove him to pleasure himself at night. Even after coming, he would have wet dreams with powerful releases that forced him to call out. He worried Lydia could hear him through the thin wall that separated their minuscule berths.

He took a swallow of the overly sweet wine. What he really should have was a bracing cup of tea, but at this hour, he doubted that could be arranged, so he drank more port. The cloyingly sweet flavor improved with each sip.

They both finally caught their breath, and Breckenridge gave him a lovely, almost shy smile.

He chuckled at the coy look so incongruous on this pirate captain.

Breckenridge chuckled back, and soon they were laughing. Ridiculous to laugh at nothing, but it felt right at that moment. Breckenridge reached across the table and took his hand. Rhain squeezed his fingers. They leaned together for a kiss, the table edge pressing into his gut.

Without breaking the kiss, his pirate climbed over the table and straddled his lap, wrapped his legs around his waist, and ground their lips and crotches together.

Breathless from the kiss, Rhain struggled to his feet, one hand on the table to steady himself, the other on the captain's firm arse to keep him in place. He made it to the bed without dropping his precious bundle and then set him gently on the mattress. Leaning over, he pushed and followed the man's controlled fall to the quilted bedding. The bed was firm and didn't give when both their weights came down together.

Holding the captain, he straightened them on the bed and, leaning on an elbow, slowly undressed them both, enjoying the perfect, almost hairless body revealed by the bright dinner lanterns still burning. Such a luxury.

His pirate lay quietly, staring at his face. The moment was potent, intimate. More intimate than the fucking he'd participated in before with unknown men who sold their arses for coin. More intimate than his lovemaking with Robert, who by comparison seemed stiff and hesitant and who allowed no illumination during their time together.

He kissed those lovely lips gently. Pulling away reluctantly, their lips held together for a second longer as if they too did not want the contact to end. "You are beautiful, my pirate."

Breckenridge smiled and ran a finger down Rhain's cheek. "As are you, my aristocrat."

Rhain laughed, trying to cover the giddy flood of contentment. "Hardly an aristocrat. I'm thirty-second in line to inherit the title *His Grace* the Duke of Portland. Not likely to ever be invited to the palace for dinner."

"The...*the* Prime Minister." Breckenridge whistled one long, low note. "How the bloody hell am I supposed to address you, then?" He didn't wait for Rhain to comment. "I have never come all over anyone related to a damn duke before."

They both laughed, but even with the jesting, he couldn't help but enjoy the surge of dizzy happiness that tickled his body like he'd swallowed a barrel of sunshine. Could Breckenridge feel how the interaction between them was something rare, something to be cherished? All at once the situation seemed too intense. He needed time to sort himself out, along with his emotions, so he turned the encounter back to the physical and licked one small dusky nipple.

Breckenridge arched off the bed and moaned. "God, do that again."

Rhain followed his orders, and soon he licked and touched all the lovely burnished skin exposed to the night air. He reached down and caressed that perfect prick, but he desired, *needed*, more. Would the captain let him? There were men who didn't partake of the ultimate sin. In fact, he'd only ever agreed to have it done to him once, when he was too soused to care. Even with the alcohol as lubrication, it had hurt like the man used a scrub brush.

Wincing at the memory, he persisted; after all, some men did seem to like being fucked. He slipped a hand under the captain's tight balls.

The man bucked his hips.

Then he slid his fingers slowly, softly along the man's arse crease.

Breckenridge gasped, opened eyes that had been squeezed shut, and pinned him with a stare. Black eyes glittering in the lamplight.

"Would you... That is, I'd like to... Well, damnation, what I'm trying to say is, will you let me fuck you?"

Smiling, Breckenridge nodded very slightly, but his body relaxed into the bedding as if he'd just been given a dram of opium. "Grab the oil from the table."

Not giving him a chance to change his mind, Rhain climbed off the bed, reached the two feet to the table, and jumped back to the bed with only half a second between.

Breckenridge laughed. "Eager, are you?" The pirate must be eager too, for he hadn't moved. There he lay with his legs cocked and spread, his dusky crease barely visible under a tight, lightly haired sac.

It took a few deep breaths before he could say, "Oh yes, I am." He slicked his fingers and slid them to the puckered hole that would soon accept his cock. He slipped in the tip of one finger. "God, you're tight, and I can feel you kissing my finger."

His pirate jerked, gasped, and looked at him with wide eyes. Did he not like bed talk, or was his arse that sensitive? Either situation could be cured by distracting him with more kisses while his hole was being prepared.

He leaned down and slipped his tongue between kiss-swollen lips just as his finger breached the tight ring of muscles. He could taste the captain's moan and feel the intimate kiss grasping and releasing his finger.

His balls screamed for release, and he had to move his hips away from the hot body next to him before he sank his ready-to-explode cock deep into this willing man.

Then, forgetting to be quiet, he told Breckenridge everything he planned to do to his body seconds before he did them. "I'm going to slip another finger into that hot hole of yours. Let your muscles play with them, stroke them, hold them tight."

Breckenridge writhed on the bed, panting. His cock bobbed up and then against his flat belly with need.

"Yes, just like that. Are you feeling full?"

The other man nodded.

"Not as full as you will feel when I put my big rod up your hole and plow you into the bed."

"Now, do it now. I'm ready."

"No, I don't believe so." Although it took everything within him to keep from taking this man right that moment, Rhain wanted him to enjoy this coupling, and that meant getting him properly prepared. "Not until your arse has kissed three of my fingers. You don't want to miss that sensation, do you?"

The captain writhed when a third finger pressed against that sweet, puckered flesh and called out as fingers pushed into the warm, tight heat.

Rhain rested his head on the other man's chest and focused on breathing and not coming. The night air whispering through the open mullioned window cooled the moisture on the tip of his cock.

There seemed to be a direct line of sensation from his fingers, being milked by anal muscles, to his cock. He could feel himself plowing Breckenridge even though his cock only touched cool air.

Trying to ignore that part of his body, his fingers fucked Breckenridge, fast, probably too fast, even though the man didn't protest, to prepare him for penetration.

"I'm going to… Unhgh." He fought back the need to release. "Are you ready for me?"

"Yes, God yes, Morgan…Rhain. Now. Do it now, Rhain."

The sound of his given name, quietly slipping between his pirate's perfect lips, sent his cock twitching. He bit his lip to keep from coming. When again in control, he positioned himself above his pirate, who wrapped his legs around his waist. Pulling out his fingers and rubbing some of the remaining oil onto his shaft, he then quickly lined up his cock to that puckering hole and pushed.

The surge of sensation, like a balloon of pleasure expanding inside his belly, was near excruciating. He bit his lip again to stay in control.

Breckenridge grabbed his arse and pulled, which seated his cock balls-deep. "God above, holy mother… *Ahhh!*" And then he pumped as if his salvation depended on a deep, hard, fast fuck.

The sound of flesh slapping flesh and arse sucking and lapping on cock filled the room. Breckenridge pulled him closer, and he felt the man's straining prick against his stomach.

"Yes, that's good. There, fuck me. Like that. Harder. Yes…yes…oh God, yes." The captain held them together with strong arms and legs as he found his release.

Looking into the captain's eyes while that hot, tight friction caressed his prick and the ship rolled from one side to the other was beyond any encounter he'd ever experienced. He was lost in that obsidian gaze as his body went over the edge of a waterfall of bliss.

ALASTAIR COULD NO more take his gaze off that handsome face with the soulful whiskey-colored eyes than he could stop his body from breathing. Sweat glistened on the pale skin and started to slick down Rhain's brown hair.

His hole burned, but the pain was nothing compared to the incomparable sensation of that big ruddy cock poking his prostate. His muscles flexed and grabbed at the cock as if they were trying to keep Rhain deep inside him forever. He moaned, because goddamn, this felt so perfect.

He pulled Rhain farther down on top of him. It restricted the man's thrusts, but Alastair needed to feel his full weight when he came.

The man was big, and that hot, heavy weight plowing him into the mattress and trapping his cock between their bodies was heaven.

Rhain would come soon, he could tell by the short rapid thrusts and the hitch in his breath. Wanting to come while being plowed, he rubbed his cock against Rhain's lightly furred abdomen. With his arse getting a thorough reaming and his cock sliding in the sweat between their bodies, his spending was imminent. He started making demands, not at all certain what he said, and then he came, pulling Rhain closer as if that could keep the man tethered inside him forever. Throwing his head back, he yelled his pleasure as thousands of exhilarating pinpricks engulfed his body.

He still enjoyed the undulating wave of pleasure coursing through his body when Rhain's thrusts lost their rhythm and his body stiffened. The tendons in his neck stood out, and his handsome face twisted as if in pain. And then he roared his pleasure.

It was the most beautiful thing he'd ever beheld.

Slowly, Rhain began to relax, and Alastair accepted all his weight. The heavy, warm, slick and sticky cocoon around him was comforting and erotic as all hell. It took only moments before he was hard again.

When Rhain's breathing went back to normal, he rose up on his arms. "I must be half suffocating you. I'll—"

"No, I love the feel of you, Rhain." And he reached for a kiss that lingered, slow and tender. A kiss like that, the feeling it left, could bring a man as weak as himself to tears.

With passion spent, they took time touching and exploring, and before long, Rhain was hard inside his arse again.

"I don't even remember your given name," Rhain whispered.

"Alastair. My name is Alastair."

Shifting his weight, Rhain lifted an arm and gently ran a finger along his overly sensitized collarbone. "Alastair. A lovely name for a beautiful man."

Staring at this strong man while his arse was stuffed full with his prick filled him with a joy and longing he never expected.

This time their loving turned slow, intimate. Rhain whispered the most outrageous things in his ear, punctuated by his given name. Each utterance sent his cock one step closer to peaking.

What was it about this man? He seemed to understand everything Alastair wanted and needed even better than he did himself. The man was a pure magician in bed.

Alastair came with Rhain's tongue twined around his. Their loving built slowly to a blinding climax that seemed to last years. His contractions around Rhain's cock, his "kisses" as Rhain called them, pushed the younger man over the threshold. He felt another surge of warm come filling his body, and at that moment, for some reason, he felt like crying.

What a bloody, damn, stupid thing. He turned his head away from Rhain's panting breaths, and as soon as the man settled from his climax, Alastair pushed at his chest.

"So sorry. You must be half flat by now." He rolled over and wiped sweat from his brow.

Alastair went to the washstand and dipped in two small towels. "This will be cold," he said as he tossed it to Rhain. When they were both clean, he slipped back into bed, and Rhain pulled him close. The boy was asleep in moments, but Alastair lay there, his head on that lightly furred, muscular chest, listening to a strong, even heartbeat, and wondered at his sudden melancholy mood.

Chapter Six

There was an amazing aroma. Spicy and dark, like a deep earthen cave. It twined around in Rhain's dreams until he woke, perhaps just to find out what produced that delightful smell.

Rhain stretched and worked his muscles, suddenly realizing he felt good. Very good.

His feet didn't hang off the side of a small bunk for the first time in… How long? Blinking one eye open, he noticed soft white-linen sheets instead of coarse stained ones, polished, stained-wood walls, instead of his unfinished pine, and enough light filtered in that there must be a window. Not his berth. *Where the devil am I?*

All of a sudden he remembered.

Damnation.

He turned over so fast the blankets moved with him, and he caught a distinct draft along his backside.

Blinking sleep from his eyes and fumbling with the blankets, it took him a moment to notice Alastair sitting calm and quiet at the table where, the night before, Rhain had intended on having a late night snack and ended up getting his cock sucked instead. There were stacks of maps and charts in front of the captain, and he stared directly at where Rhain had just covered his naked arse. His face heated.

"Good morning. Did you sleep well?" Alastair said with a half smile and one raised brow.

Rhain buried his head in the blankets for a moment, but couldn't keep from chuckling. "Yes, surprising with all the noise on this ship. How can you sleep through all those damn bells that ring all day and all night?"

The bed dipped, and Rhain forced away his embarrassment. Uncomfortable lazing about when Alastair was up and dressed and sitting so close he could feel the heat against his hip, he uncovered and sat up.

"Actually, the bells help me sleep. They tell me that all is well, what time it is, and that assigned duties are being seen to."

"All that information from annoying bells?"

"They only ring every half hour. *Not* all day and all night." Brushing back that coquettish braid, Alastair smiled a gentle, almost shy smile.

Shy was not a reaction he ever thought to see on this man's face. It suited him. It suited him very well.

"Would you like to break your fast? We have eggs and sausage, very dry bread. I wouldn't suggest eating that. It is hard enough to break a tooth." He stood and thumped the pale, round loaf on the table to demonstrate. "And there is this strange brew that cook makes. We received a cask full of cocoa—awful stuff—in Venezuela about two years ago. I do not care for the damn dark, bitter beans. Cook tried at least a dozen ways to prepare it where it would be palatable to me, since the locals swear it has nourishing properties and we have so much of it. All his attempts were dreadful, except this one." He walked over to the bed, holding out a cup of what looked like normal hot chocolate but smelled like a rich field. "Want to try it?"

Nodding, he took the cup.

"I have to warn you, there is enough sugar in that cup to choke a cow."

"I should like it, then. Lydia complains that I eat up all the sweets in the house before she has an opportunity to try them." He took a sip of the piquant and very sweet drink. It was good. It was...better than good. Not fantastic—too unusual for that—but addictive to be sure. He took another sip to verify his assessment. "This is good. I'd like to buy the ingredients from you. As long as they come with the recipe for this drink." He held up the cup and took a deep swallow, allowing the liquid to sit heavy and thick on his tongue.

"My dear, I will give you a bag of those damnable beans along with the dried chilies and cardamom that make them tolerable." He extracted the cup from Rhain's hand and leaned in for a kiss.

The kiss tasted like the drink—dark and sinful. He felt his rod stirring, even though he'd experienced four extraordinary orgasms the night before.

When Alastair pulled back, his eyes were simmering with lust. "Currently, I have to plot a course to Barbados. Something I find rather tedious and have performed since my sailing master decided not to leave Morocco."

"You do? I think it would be fascinating. It is something I would enjoy learning more about."

His captain rose, lifted a dust-covered tome, and handed it to Rhain. "This is a text on navigation. Feel free to borrow it. I have not looked at the dry thing in years. I shall warn you, however, it will put you in a doze faster than a full bottle of wine."

Rhain looked at the old book and thumbed through a few pages. It seemed like something he would enjoy. There were equations, star charts, and diagrams he did not as of yet understand but was looking forward to learning more about them. He looked at Alastair and said, "Thank you."

Alastair looked away. "Yes, well, I must work, but do feel free to eat and walk around my cabin naked as long as you'd like." He swatted Rhain's thigh and left the bed to return to his charts.

Rhain laughed. "But what about my reputation if it were to become known that you have seen my cock, sir?"

"Rhain, I do believe that with the roaring you did last night, the crew knows you plowed me. If they are not shocked at that, they will not be shocked with a simple ogling of your interesting regions." He winked.

Something deep inside him twisted and changed during their teasing. Rhain had the sneaking suspicion he genuinely liked his pirate.

* * * *

It took him almost half an hour to leave the captain's chamber.

Alastair insisted Rhain needed help with his jacket, his shirt, his cravat. The longest delay was when he'd required help with his drawers. Oh Lord, the way he helped with those drawers.

Rhain walked awkwardly, the stiffening cock in his trousers responding to the memory of Alastair giving him what he called "an olive oil cleansing."

He stopped for a second, leaned against a large crate, and breathed. Staring up at the light clouds overhead, he managed to force his prick and his desires to rest.

By the location of the sun, it must be close to the noon hour. That would explain why he didn't have a bad head after all the port he'd consumed last night.

He would make it to his room. He would bathe, as best he could with the ewer of salt water he received every morning, and then he would... He would what? He'd written all the letters he needed to send before leaving England. He had no occupation on ship. He'd already read everything there was to read on running plantations and on curing diseases that exhibit a consumptive habit. What could he do?

He knew what he would like to keep doing, but unfortunately, the captain had duties.

Perhaps he could learn something about sailing or read the book on navigation.

"Rhain."

He turned at Lydia's cry.

Wearing a cotton dress and gloves, she sat crossed-legged in the sun, twining rope together in an intricate fashion. Each strand of jute looked as big around as her delicate fingers.

He walked over. "Of course you know you will ruin all your clothing before we reach Dominica, do you not?"

The imp shrugged. Something the sailors must have taught her, along with rope splicing. "Good morning to you, brother; did you sleep well?" She had the devil's own twinkle in her eyes.

He sat down next to her, not nearly as graceful as she, as he couldn't even comprehend getting his legs twisted up into that position. "I was, umm, conversing with—"

"Don't even try to prevaricate, Rhain. I know where you were. All night long and all morning."

He felt himself blush. "It was important to—"

"And I know what you were doing. I'm surprised you're hiding it; you know I won't judge you."

He wrapped one arm around her and gave her a quick hug. "Lydia, I don't know what I ever did to deserve you as a sister."

She smiled up at him. "Why, I think I'm the one who got the best hand of cards. I've never met any other brothers who would tend to a sick and opinionated little brat as unquestioningly as you have, my dear." Looking down at the rope to continue the tedious—and to him incomprehensible—process of splicing in a new length of jute, she whispered, "I'm glad you stayed with him. I think he will be good for you, Rhain. After all, you have not had anyone who cared for you since Robert, and he was only bearable part of the time."

"Lydia."

"No, please listen, and don't disregard this. You deserve to be happy with someone who will take care of you as you have always taken care of everyone else."

"That is not true."

"Yes it is. Father would have succumbed to despair after Mother died if you hadn't kept him from dwelling in his misery for the rest of his life, and then you started taking care of me. And you so young." Eyes downcast, she shook her head slowly, then said, "Just let this thing happen between you and the captain. See where it goes."

"It will end as soon as we land in Dominica, if not sooner; you know that, Lyd."

She looked at him with lips puckered and shook her head. "I wish you would stop being so black and white and enjoy the grays for once in your life."

"Why do people keep saying that to me?" he grumbled.

"Perhaps because you need to hear it, brother of mine."

He patted her knee, his cupped palm making a popping sound on the smooth cotton, and then rose from the scrubbed wooden decking. "Thank you for your blessing, Lyd. I think I can promise you that currently I'm very much enjoying the grays." He left her to her splicing and couldn't seem to stop smiling as he went belowdeck.

* * * *

Dunn stood over Alastair with a very big smirk. Actually, he'd come into the captain's chamber smirking, smirked through the whole dialogue about their need to stop for more supplies because the easterlies had been against them the whole time, and pronounced this would likely delay them by another sennight.

Alastair was getting right and tired of the smirk. "Out with it, Dunn."

The man's lips trembled as he spoke. "Have a good time with the nob, sir?"

"Quite nice. But I don't see how that's any of your business."

"No, sir. None of my business for a certainty, sir." Dunn nearly choked on a chuckle.

"I find it hard to understand what you think is so funny at the moment. Please do enlighten me."

"Oh, it is nothing. Nothing at all, sir… Except, I believe, you were under the impression that I would prick the nob girl before you had a chance to soften up and prick the nob boy."

Alastair waved that nonsense off. "Not at all, not at all. Because you see, I was not the one doing the pricking."

Dunn lost his composure at that and roared with laughter.

Holding back his own mirth as best he could, he waited until his first mate got himself under control. "Our delay in Morocco ate into our profits, but perhaps we can pick up some extra trade in Dominica."

"Hmm, yes. Haven't heard that their goods are worth much the past few years, Captain, but we can carry sugar. That is always of interest in Boston Town and London."

With a shift as fast as a waterspout, Dunn changed topics. "I hope we can make up time. Would be nice to spend some time in my little house this trip."

Alastair absentmindedly drew circles on the tabletop with one finger as he listened to Dunn prattle on. The first mate had purchased a small plot of land and a home a few miles outside of Boston Town two years ago, with plans to retire and try his hand at farming. Someplace close to water so he could hop on a boat if he needed a taste of the sea. So far he'd only been able to check on the place once a year to make certain the caretaker managed it well.

The room went quiet.

Alastair looked up.

"Captain."

"Hmm?"

Dunn's expression turned serious as he pushed a lock of dark hair off his forehead. "We've been in the doldrums since last night and before that a few days of the easterlies. We should have stopped at the Canaries for provisions."

Nodding and fighting the prickle of unease, he handed Dunn the day's navigation plan and said, "Set a course, then, in case we catch a wind."

"Captain?"

"What now, Dunn?"

"You will tell Mr. Morgan, then? Since the two of you are so close, that is."

Alastair sighed and straightened a pile of smooth parchment. "Stop smirking, or I'll make you tell the uptight Mr. Morgan."

"Aye, sir."

The insufferable first mate left, but the sound of his laughter could be heard through the closed door.

Chapter Seven

Later that day—the surprising part of the day—Rhain was pleasant and didn't seem to mind the delay.

"Rhain?"

"Yes?"

"You do realize this will delay us reaching Dominica? Last time we were stuck in the doldrums, we spun around in circles for ten days. We will start rationing immediately in case we have similarly bad luck."

"Ten days?" The young man shrugged one powerful shoulder. "Well, there isn't anything we can do, I suppose, so we might as well enjoy the trip, even with empty bellies. I mean… God, man, just look at that beautiful blue expanse and the light, fluffy clouds. So peaceful. I see why sailors take to the seas."

Rhain had been on his ship for more than two fortnights, and he just now noticed the allure of the ocean? The man seemed relaxed for the first time since Alastair met him. He left off the coat and leaned against the bulwark cap in shirt sleeves, brown hair ruffled by the clement ocean breeze, slight smile playing across wide, kissable lips. In this moment, he was beyond beautiful; ten rungs above handsome. He wanted him again; right here, right now, on the main deck, in front of his crew and God. The raging desire in his gut made him take a step closer without conscious thought. "Rhain, dine with me again tonight."

The boy closed his eyes as if comparing what he wanted with what he knew to be right, then gave one decisive nod before the smile on his face grew to a full happy-to-be-alive smile. He turned, and whiskey-brown eyes stared directly at Alastair. "I'd like that, pirate. I'd like that very much."

Well, I'll be… Guess the man just needed a dab of buggery now and again to set his personality to rights. Pirate, hmmm? Yes, he most certainly liked the content, less prickly Rhain. He liked him immensely.

He took a huge lungful of fresh sea air and anticipated his evening.

RHAIN WATCHED THE pirate walk away and then climb the stairs to the quarterdeck. The tight, worn buckskin breeches clung to his perfect arse like a lover's touch. So rare to see a firm, neat waist flare just the right amount to make the transition from lower back to strong buttocks and thighs. One of God's masterpieces instead of a mere backend. He sighed again. Damn, but he felt good with the clean smell of the salty breeze on his face, unfiltered through coal soot, the warmth of the sun on his shoulders, the sound of a sail snapping as it filled with air, and seamen cheering at the gust of wind.

A warm buzz fluttered low in his abdomen, and a slow, lazy feeling he'd not felt in… Well, years in fact.

He smiled again, his face muscles aching from overuse. He wished to throw his head back and laugh just because he could do it without faking happiness for the first time since Lydia contracted her illness. He didn't laugh only because he would look like a fool.

All this contentment and a dark, sensual pirate possibly for an extra ten days. Now they had around a month left on ship. He had at least thirty more days in a safe place where he and his pirate could fashion memories. Enough memories to store up and take out miserly when he needed confirmation that at one time he'd been desired for himself and had fully acted upon that desire.

These memories would see him through the rest of his celibate life. For a moment that thought threatened to overwhelm him, but he forced the black wave of despair away and remembered his vow from late last night: he would continue his celibacy once off this ship, but this time he would control the urge and be fully celibate until his death.

He'd decided he would not wed. He could not do that, knowing his preference for men was so strong.

No one on the island would learn of his debauched crossing, and as long as he had this month with his pirate—and he would embrace each and every day with both hands, both legs, his emotions, and his prick—then he could return to his safe but celibate life.

A surge of desire raced up his legs and touched every fiber of his body, from toes to fingers and everything in between.

He scanned the deck, looking for Lydia, but didn't see her. Instead he saw a large man staring right at him. That in and of itself was not unusual. First Mate Dunn told him the interest in them stemmed from the sailors not being used to landlubbers on the ship. What was unusual—and this stood out to Rhain—was the glare on the man's sun-browned face and his whispering to an equally angry-looking friend.

A small cough behind him made him jump, so absorbed he'd been in ferreting out why these men were unhappy.

"Is it not a perfect day, dear brother?" Lydia said, her voice clear and free from the congestion that plagued her since her nineteenth year.

"Yes, perfect, and you seem much improved. Very good to see you pink-cheeked and smiling."

She laughed. "It is wonderful to feel well enough to enjoy myself. Thank you." In a fashion so unlike her, she threw her arms around him in a spontaneous hug.

He squeezed her back.

"Is there not any way we can stay on this boat forever? The air is so clean, I feel as though I can breathe enough of it for every soul in London." She squeezed with all her slight strength and then let him go.

"Very pleased to give you the good news, sister. We are delayed, and it will be no earlier than thirty days before we must leave the *Hurricane.*"

"Truly?"

"Yes, truly."

"Oh, how lovely. Lovely indeed. I must go tell First Mate Dunn. He will be pleased."

He put a hand on her sleeve. "Dear, I'm certain he was one of the first to know."

"Oh, right. How stupid of me. I suppose... I suppose I am just so giddy from the news." She beamed beautifully. Her unruly curls slipped from their pins, losing the battle against the sea air.

"I am going to find him anyway. I like him, and I want to enjoy feeling young and healthy, while I feel healthy. And I think you should..." She stopped and scanned the ship until she spotted the pirate. "You should enjoy your captain's attentions as long as we are here. He likes you, I can tell. And you like him. Don't be daft and allow this time to be wasted." She, his young sister, grabbed his arm and told him, "Nothing you can be responsible for while on this boat, so enjoy your freedom and enjoy your pirate." She skipped away, giggling, before he could grab her and tell her to be careful.

He laughed at her antics and then looked up. His pirate stared at him, and lust once again blossomed inside him. He smiled, letting his pirate know his thoughts were on tonight.

Chapter Eight

They didn't make it until supper. By tea, Rhain had Alastair bent over the captain's table and tried to feel the man's tonsils with his cock by ramming it as far as he could up the man's arse. He planned to claim that perfect dusky hole so that Alastair never forgot him.

Rhain put his hand between Alastair's shoulders and forced him against the dark, stained tabletop. Alastair turned his head, placed his cheek to the polished surface, and stretched his hands across to grasp the far edge. The view of that whipcord, tough body spread out as if in bonds set his cock to donkey-sized proportions.

"Alastair, this will be over much too soon, but I will make it up to you afterward. Is that all right with you?"

Alastair nodded and groaned when Rhain pumped with whirlwind speed.

The climax shot through him like lightning fire through a haystack. His vision blacked, and his legs buckled. Supporting himself with a hand on the table, he stayed there, cock in his lover's arse, until all the glorious contractions subsided and he could actually see again.

Pulling out slowly, he ran light caresses down Alastair's long lean back.

The man sighed quietly, and his arse hole winked at him.

"Can you make it to the bed, or should I carry you?"

Alastair laughed. "I'm going; just give me a moment." He stood slowly as if his arse were sore, but his cock jutted full and bold and pointing to the ceiling.

When his lover sprawled on the rumpled sheets, Rhain climbed onto the foot of the bed and crawled up that gorgeous body until his mouth was level with that pretty, long prick. He took one long moment to breathe in the smell of aroused male laced with wintergreen and the scent of sunshine.

Alastair traced his fingers through Rhain's hair. "So soft. Such a rich color, I think it could warm my fingers on a cold night." The questing fingers caressed his cheek, then his lips, in a gesture so loving, Rhain briefly contemplated running from the room.

Fighting the impulse, he decided to embrace the intimacy and see where it would lead them. He leaned down and captured the tip of

Alastair's cock while gazing into ocean-deep black eyes. Alastair pushed up gently as Rhain engulfed the iron-hard rod.

The flavor was amazingly arousing. He'd always enjoyed sucking men off, but no one had ever tasted like this—clean outdoors and masculine strength. He could stay here forever, with his mouth full, his nose inhaling heaven, and gazing at one of the loveliest men he could ever remember seeing.

Alastair twined his fingers into Rhain's hair but never pulled, never forced. He pumped his hips in time with Rhain's rhythm but never shoved himself in or choked Rhain with a surprise lunge.

In essence, he was the most considerate man he'd ever lain with. And that scared the ever living hell out of him. His heart started doing all kinds of funny trips and lurches, the damn organ.

For such a vibrant man, who yelled and bellowed and demanded outside the bedroom, he was a quiet, gentle lover. The dichotomy proved to be an unexpected stimulant. He would come again just by sucking Alastair and rubbing against the bedding.

Nearly over the top already, he increased his pressure on Alastair's cock. The change in position caused a slurping noise more exciting than a hand to his own prick.

They came together, gazes locked, breaths raspy, muscles tensing. Rhain didn't cry out only because his mouth was full of cock and come.

Alastair moaned and then sighed. "Rhain."

Damn, but he loved the sound of his name on this man's lips.

He milked Alastair's cock until it started to soften and no more come leaked out.

"Come up here," Alastair said quietly.

He settled beside the lithe, long body and pulled Alastair close so he could rest his head on Rhain's chest. Stroking a hand slowly up and down his lover's back, he thought Alastair had fallen asleep, when he said, "I do not mean to pry, but I must know something. I expected Miss Lydia to be viper-spitting angry today. She was not. Instead she gave me more smiles and 'good days' than she has before. The girl even teased me. Teased."

Stroking Alastair's sweat-dampened hair behind one ear, he said, "She knows my preferences."

"And she accepts this? How is that so?"

"It happened so slowly, I'm not exactly certain when she fully comprehended what it meant that I slept with other men. For so long she would encourage my attention to certain boys I would bring home from school for the holidays and away from others she didn't like. She would put it something like, 'He is not good enough for you, Rhain.' That slowly turned into more forward statements like, 'He is much more handsome than your other friend. You will like him better, I think.' Then one day I found that she and I were wondering if we should invite a particular friend of mine to move into our guest chamber."

"Astounding."

"Yes, Lydia is that." He smiled. "The best parts were that I never had to lie to her, and when she fended off marriage-minded women. One time, she convinced a very persistent Miss Mary Thompson that I would not suit because I was a bear in the morning and yelled at everyone until afternoon tea."

Alastair smiled and touched his shoulder. "How very fortunate you were."

Rhain nodded and truly agreed.

"So tell me how someone who is thirty-second in line to a dukedom has a Welsh name?"

Snorting, Rhain rolled his eyes. "My father was half Welsh. Mother's family almost disowned her when she ran off and married him. To show her displeasure, she named her first child—me—after my paternal grand-uncle. Had a few fights at school because some people didn't think my blood was English enough."

"I imagine you won all those fights."

That bit of flattery warmed him. He kissed Alastair's nose gently. "And what about you?"

Nodding, his pirate told the tale of his life. "Father was in the British navy, worked his way up to first mate. When their ship captured a French frigate, he gained his captaincy. Did a bit of privateering on the side, which gave him enough funds and a prize ship to start his own shipping line. He owns a small fleet based in Boston Town. Mother refused to leave London. I visit them both when I'm in port. I plan to purchase a few more ships in the future. Build my own fleet. One of these days.

"There, my boring story has been shared, so tell me what I really want to know." Alastair gave him a slow, deep kiss. "It is obvious you know your way around a man's body, so these friends were past lovers. Tell me about them?"

Rhain laughed. "It is not a pretty tale. I'd rather not."

But when Alastair propped his chin on his chest and gazed at him with those dark eyes, he found he wished to tell him everything.

"There were a number of school friends with whom I exchanged hand and sucking pleasures. We were all in a perpetual state of arousal back then, so I don't know if any of them shared the same proclivities that I...that we share. None of us ever shared anal penetration, but then I was so ignorant, I didn't even know at the time a person could do that."

Alastair chuckled and fondled his chest hair, twining a few strands around his finger and then untwining it.

"Then there was Robert. We met at my gentlemen's club. He was—I suppose still is—an athletic man, and we had many things in common. He is a year older than me. Had a year or two more experience. He let me... Well, he actually taught me how to..." He waved a hand over Alastair's body as if that would convey the embarrassment of his first time, but Alastair nodded as if he understood.

"He was like you. He liked to..." Again, he waved his hand over his and Alastair's bodies. "God, I am miserable at this."

"He liked to be the one receiving."

Rhain nodded. "We knew each other for a year before we became lovers, during which I fell hopelessly in love. He did too, I believe, at least half in love, anyway. When we began our affair, he was so frightened of being caught, we weren't able to come together as often as I wished."

"What happened?"

"He wed. Lydia thought we should murder him in his sleep. I thought that was over the top, so we succeeded in drinking ourselves into an inebriated state instead." He shrugged, ready for this conversation to be over.

"Hard to imagine your sister in her cups, but I'm happy she was there for you. That must have been difficult."

"Yes."

Alastair must have realized he no longer wished to talk. He laid his head back on Rhain's chest and started sharing his own history. "I suppose you might think I'm a bad man. I've had lots of experience. I started at fourteen. One of my father's friends. It was wonderful, and I never told Father. It lasted about six months, and then I apprenticed on one of Father's ships, and that was that. We would occasionally have a quick fuck when I returned to Boston, but that stopped after his fall into laziness. I wasn't interested any longer. Plus, I knew where to find younger men at that point."

Alastair gave a brief kiss to his nipple. The sizzle of sensation made him jump.

"Being at sea, traveling all the time, makes it difficult to become involved with anyone. I've fucked plenty of men, but never had anyone special to me."

"Good for you. You can't be hurt that way."

"You think so?"

He nodded.

"I don't know. I think it is a bit sad." He placed his hand over Rhain's heart. "Actually, it is very sad."

Sad. He lifted the man's chin and placed a small kiss on his lips. "I don't want you to be sad. What can I do to make you feel happy?"

"You could fuck me again."

"God, you are insatiable."

Alastair smiled wickedly. "We have so little time before Dominica; must make the best out of having two troublesome nobs on board."

Rhain laughed. "Just for that comment, I'm going to treat you like the lowly pirate you are. On your hands and knees, cur. I will teach you to keep a civil tongue in your mouth around your betters."

Alastair didn't hesitate; he positioned onto hands and knees in seconds. His dark, smooth olive skin was several shades lighter than the dark crack. Two tight muscles ran from thigh to back. Tight and taut and irresistible.

There was no need for oil or preparation. Alastair's arse gleamed from oil and come, and he was stretched and welcoming. Still, Rhain took the time to kiss both arse cheeks and slip a finger into the warm, slick hole, just as much for his pleasure as for Alastair's. And what pleasure. Fully, totally, and completely.

The buggering was rough and fast and over much too quickly.

* * * *

Rhain was in love.

Two days after they first fucked and he was already giddy with that unwanted emotion. What a goddamn worthless feeling for someone who would be out of his life before the change of seasons. But here he stood, holding the warm feeling close to his chest, enjoying the familiar light-headed surges.

The emotion sneaked up on him so slowly, he almost didn't recognize it. But then last night, under the cover of candlelight, with Alastair's supple body moving in rhythm beneath him, staring at eyes black as pitch, he'd realized. In the span of a month's time, this stunningly beautiful man had captured his heart as well as his desires.

It wasn't just one thing; there were so many elements that made up the person he loved. His compassion for a motley, diverse crew, his ability to demand acceptance in each and every man and the odd woman under his command, his wit, his beauty...

Feeling like a lovestruck youngster, he forced his attention to the churning water and foam forming behind the ship as they slipped ever closer to Dominica. The doldrums only lasted two days. The delay only two days, not ten.

Every hour they sailed was one hour closer to Dominica, the port where he would leave his love, perhaps to never see the vibrant man again. No, he corrected himself. He definitely would never see Alastair again. There would be no point.

What good would it do to open up the wound once every few years when some shipment brought him close enough to visit Dominica's main port, Roseau, for a day or two? That would be beyond painful.

Better to cut all ties, and now that he knew what intercourse with another man could really offer, he realized he could not be celibate. He would continue his occasional visit to molly houses to slake his lust. And at night, now he would have memories more vibrant than Robert's tepid efforts.

He pulled out an old, well-worn piece of paper and ran a thumb over one of the many creases. He'd held on to this letter for—what was it, a full year now? He would no longer need to pull out the sad little reminder of his failed relationship with Robert, the only other man he had loved. He would never again read the letter, touch himself, and occasionally cry himself to sleep.

In fact, he'd not read the letter in months. Had almost forgotten it tucked away in a pocket in a seldom used waistcoat.

He read it one last time.

My Dear RM,

I am a coward of the worst order.

The way I have chosen to inform you of my decision is unforgivable, but I find I am unable to broach the subject while in the same room with you. It is those big brown eyes of yours, you see. They can always persuade me to do your bidding. Always have. Nearly got me in trouble many times over the past two years.

But this… What should I call it, attraction? It cannot continue. I do not know what happened to alert him, but I think my brother suspects. With his loathing of me, he will certainly cause us problems if he finds proof. Imagine what my parents would say if they were told.

I have decided to move forward with my engagement to Violet. The wedding will be in June. Please do not come.

You have been the best of friends these past two years. I would do nothing to hurt you if I could avoid it, but you know as well as I that we cannot be together.

Do not fret over this, for you will soon find someone who loves you as you deserve. I hope you let me share in your joy on that day.

Your friend always,

R

Robert had been a good friend, but their broken liaison made a hash of that. The letter had been the last he heard from Robert. He wasn't even certain if the man's marriage bore fruit and produced a grandchild he knew Robert's mother so coveted. Not that it mattered. He no longer desired Robert's pale-blond hair and insipid gray eyes.

With sure, steady hands, he flung the letter into the wind which filled the sails again since that morning, and watched it flutter up and away to land somewhere in the blue, blue Atlantic Ocean.

* * * *

"Enter." Alastair studied a route map to help with the plotting of their next course. He should have done this already, but he spent so much time in bed with Rhain the past few weeks, that he had fallen behind on his duties. He promised Dunn that morning he would do a better job at being captain from that point further.

He almost laughed at his sorry state until he looked at his visitor. Standing in front of his desk, legs spread for balance and possibly to also showcase his package, was Balls. The man was big, filling a large part of the captain's cabin. He was bold, with long, loose brown hair swept back from a handsome face and tall forehead.

Even after a long night of passion, this man was able to elicit arousal. "What do you want, Balls?"

"Moment of your time, Captain." The words were spun with desire.

"As you can see, I have very little of that commodity at the moment." He waved at the maps on the table. "Why not take up your concerns with First Mate Dunn?"

"He cain't help with the problem I have."

Hating to ask but knowing that would be the best way to rid himself of this man, he said, "Right, then, what is your issue?"

"This, sir." Then the large man stroked the front of his breeches, and a fully impressive cockstand filled the man's hand.

He swallowed the saliva flooding his mouth, took a deep breath, and then looked away.

"It has been a long voyage, Captain. Ain't no one on ship who is desirable as you." Then he whispered in a low, husky growl, "I need you, sir. Need you bad."

Alastair refused to look at the tempting offer.

"Cain't do me duty if I'm dangling for you day and night, now can I?" He leaned over the table and placed a large hand on Alastair's shoulder, running a few fingers along his neck. "I have missed you somethin' fierce."

"Enough. Take yourself belowdeck and find a willing body. I am certain there are plenty willing to"—he nodded at the impressive bulge in Balls's breeches—"sample that."

"I need *you*, sir. Only you writhing under me can solve my problem." He pulled Alastair closer.

Alastair stood, knocking over his chair, and said very slowly and very quietly, "I said that was enough. Remove yourself now, or prepare yourself to be locked up. Do I make myself clear?"

Balls made for the door, stomping like a four-year-old child. He turned and said, "It is because of that fancy bit you got in your bed these days, isn't it? 'Cause I can outdo anything he—"

"Out. Now!"

The man left, but not before tossing over his shoulder, "You will regret this." And then he gave a sloppy salute and tramped away.

Regret not taking the man up on his offer? Not likely when he had a much more handsome, much more agreeable lover at the moment.

He sighed. What had he ever seen in Balls?

Chapter Nine

Everyone was on deck, watching the green horizon of Barbados grow in their view. Apparently even hardened seamen got tired of nothing but blue three hundred and sixty degrees around the boat. Thirty-three days since they last set foot on land, and the green horizon beckoned to his soul.

The past week their water tasted so bad, Rhain lost his desire to drink, and the food was nothing more than dried provisions that all tasted like wood shavings.

Lydia squeezed his arm and pointed at a large white-and-gray seabird skimming over their spot by the rail so quietly it didn't seem real.

The bird was close enough he could see a small but intelligent eye considering them. To the bird, they must all seem like clumsy flightless creatures on a floating wooden island.

"They are amazingly beautiful, Rhain. Just seeming to float on the air with no effort."

He watched the agile creature drift off to watch a group of sailors before heading toward shore. "Would you fly if you could, Lydia?" he asked.

"Oh yes. Without hesitation. To feel so free, with the wind pushing me up, farther and farther toward the clouds. What an unbelievable experience that would be." Her gaze moved up to the sun's midmorning kiss. "Would you, brother?"

Rhain glanced at the glaring sun and then back at his sister. He suspected he would not choose to fly. Not unless he were guaranteed a safe landing back on earth. "I think I would much rather watch you fly, dear." He kissed the top of her curly head.

She giggled and hugged his arm.

So different, the two of them. Lydia, frail and not expected to live to her twenty-fifth birthday, willing to embrace anything, and he…

He squinted at the bright sky, then opened his eyes fully on the breathtaking shore. He embraced what he knew. He tried to live a normal life. Would be happy to live a normal life, if he was normal. He wasn't. So how far from what he considered orthodox and safe was he willing to go?

His gaze shifted to the captain, currently at the wheel. First Mate Dunn stood next to him, performing something incomprehensible with a sextant. The pirate captain, tall and strong, guided the ship and issued orders such as "shake up the main," "keep her trimmed by the head," and other unfathomable commands.

Rhain barely recognized the words as English. He smiled. Apparently, he was willing to go quite a bit out of "normal" to gain what he truly desired. "Maybe I would take a flight with you, dear. A very short one."

After several minutes of ogling his pirate, he turned greedy eyes on the land. They occupied a prime viewing location. The captain insured they had a good spot that morning by ordering a few sun-leathered men away from the fore rail.

"Rhain, I've been able to piece together some of the captain's accounts and showed him how to keep two sets of books to trick the taxman; he was surprised by that." She laughed. "He has a problem this year. He lost contracted cargo because of his delay in Morocco, even picking up our fare—which was outrageous by the way; why didn't you tell me?"

Rhain shrugged. He hadn't wished her to worry when she learned most of their funds went to the purchase of transport.

"Well, at any rate, he found other cargo, but it was less profitable than he expected. This ship will lose money this year. I wonder if he has plans on how to make up for his shortfall?"

Hearing this news, Rhain felt guilty for his animosity over the price he paid for their voyage. If he had any of the money that some of his relatives squandered, he would offer to pay more, just to make certain Alastair did not lose his ship.

The shoreline was close enough now to distinguish a beach, shrubs, and trees. One forest-covered mountain appeared almost purple in its misty, hazed elegance.

"Oh, Rhain, I do hope our island is this beautiful."

She glowed, happy and healthy. He'd not heard a single cough in days.

Squeezing her hand resting on his arm, he said, "I'm certain it will be just as beautiful, my dear." He hoped so, for her benefit. The poor girl had suffered enough; it was time for something to go well for her.

It took almost an hour before they changed course to slip alongside the verdant shoreline, and another half hour before they moved into a cove and dropped anchor. A high bluff shaded part of the cove's clear sapphire water.

A large shirtless seaman with a long brown braid walked past, almost clipping Rhain's shoulder, and muttered, "Dragging the captain around by his prick."

Lydia gasped and spun around to confront the man, but all they saw was a retreating back, tight breeches, and the long braid swinging as he walked barefoot on the scrubbed boards.

Rhain grabbed her arm to keep her from giving chase.

"Don't, Lyd. It means nothing. He probably received some undesirable ship duty or something."

"Still. He should not treat you with such little respect."

He pulled her back to her spot by the rail and distracted her with pointing out aspects of the scenery.

As soon as the anchor held, the crew gave a hue and cry. Many men threw off their clothes and dived into the water.

Lydia laughed and clapped her hands, not even shocked by the naked flesh flashing by.

Rhain realized he smiled like an idiot, so he let himself laugh with his lovely sister and enjoyed the sight of tanned, naked men frolicking in the water. Pulling at his sea-salt-scratchy cravat, he wished he could join them.

It was midday before they climbed down into a skiff headed for shore with First Mate Dunn and four capable rowers.

The captain was still on board, organizing the land crews. The men bustled about as if the whole affair were carefully planned by a general preparing for battle. There must have been a thousand details required for restocking a ship. His pirate stood, authoritative and desirable as hell, bellowing orders while men scurried around to follow them.

Damn, he was half hard, probably due in part to the expectation of having solid land under his feet for the first time in forever. God, he could smell the earth, the vegetation. He had missed that and didn't even realize. He longed to grab a handful of sand and squeeze it between his fingers. He wanted to feel the stillness of the earth, so predictable, so safe.

When the skiff hit ground, he jumped out of the boat and lifted Lydia to keep her from soaking her clothes in the clear blue water. He nearly stumbled on the dry sand. For some strange reason, the earth seemed to sway under his feet.

A midshipman grabbed his arm and stabilized him before he dropped Lydia. "Not to worry, sir. It's the sea legs. You become used to the rocking, and then when it stops, your body keeps up the motion. You'll settle out in a day or two."

A day or two and they would be back on ship. Would he then have the same disconcerting disequilibrium when he boarded?

Lydia stumbled and then laughed. "I feel like I'm on skates for the first time and am somewhat out of control."

The first mate brought Tim over and said, "Miss Lydia, Tim here can take you over to that set of rocks, and with a blanket strung up, you can have a private bathing spot. She can also help you with your laundry. It will be perfectly safe. The men have their orders and will not bother you."

"Oh, what a lovely thought. Rhain?"

At the gleam in her eyes, all he could do was give her this boon. "Of course, Lydia. I'll bathe over there." He pointed at a spot halfway between where they stood and the rocks where she would bathe.

Without a backward glance, she picked up her laundry and grabbed Tim's hand. "Come on, then, my friend, time for a swim." The two women hurried away, with Tim looking somewhat stunned.

First Mate Dunn clapped him on the shoulder. "They'll be all right. Tim is a trustworthy hand, although I think she is half besotted with Miss Lydia already."

Rhain tensed.

"Not to worry. Tim has a girl in just about every port. She won't fall too hard." He winked, and Rhain fought the urge to follow the two women.

* * * *

With half his mind keeping watch on Lydia, he shucked his clothes and walked into the water, which felt cool against his hot skin. Sucking in a breath from the chill, he dived under to stop the slow torture of icy needles of water lapping at his skin.

Swimming warmed him up, and then the clean water felt wonderful on salt-caked skin. He stretched arms and kicked legs in a satisfying physical activity he'd not enjoyed in years. Always loving to swim, he decided that at their new home, he and Lydia would swim daily. It would be good for them. He slipped easily through the water, wondering how close their plantation home was to the ocean.

ALASTAIR WATCHED HIS lover slide gracefully through the sapphire-blue water. Large, powerful muscles propelled Rhain with little effort. Dark hair slick against his head, face beginning to tan from the sun, the man appeared positively edible.

Half an hour later, he finished his work and made his way over to where Rhain washed his clothes in the nude. His London pale skin flexing over a purely male frame was spectacular.

Most of the seamen not in the hunting party were also nude and washing either themselves or their clothing, but none of those lean, tan bodies held his interest.

"Did you enjoy your swim?" he asked as he walked toward Rhain.

The man crouched, bending toward the water where he rinsed out the last of the soap. He turned, face tinged pink, probably only partially from the sun.

Smiling, Alastair made his move. "Grab up your clothes; there is a freshwater pond not far. You can rinse out the salt to make the cloth less scratchy. I'll have Tim do the same for Miss Lydia's things in that stream over there." He pointed to the other side of the lagoon. "I see they are dressed and enjoying the sun. Mate Dunn can stay with Miss Lydia until Tim is finished."

Rhain grabbed up his wet things and casually held the wad in front of his crotch.

After Alastair made the arrangements with Tim, he showed Rhain the way to the secluded jade-green pond formed by a depression in the rocks, where a small stream flowed. The place was picturesque, and he made a point to stop here every time he came this direction. He helped Rhain rinse the clothes, and they stretched them out on short bushes, disturbing a bright-green bird in the process.

He stripped fast. He longed for fresh water and clean skin. Alastair appreciated Rhain's strong, tall body but did not give in to the temptation to touch. There was time after they went for a swim.

God, the cool fresh water felt soft against his rough, salt-encrusted skin. He took a deep breath and then sighed.

Rhain, almost shyly, lowered himself into the water. For such a domineering love partner, the man could be downright endearing with his blushes and shy glances.

Alastair swam over to him, took his lover in his arms, and kissed those beautiful lips, but Rhain frowned and pushed him away.

"Someone will see."

"Not at all. I've asked for one hour of privacy, and it will be maintained, of that you can be certain. And if someone from the ship happens to catch a glance, it will be nothing they haven't seen many times already." He reached for Rhain again, but the man swam away.

Turning over on his back, Rhain said, "I don't know. I'm not as comfortable with all this as you." He waved toward the shoreline where most of the crew gathered water from the stream.

"Rhain, I wished to show you this place. I've been planning to take you on that soft mossy spot for days. Come here." He held out his hand while treading water, and Rhain hesitated only for a moment before swimming over and giving him a bruising kiss.

In the end, Rhain took Alastair on the mossy spot. He wasn't quite certain if he was the one who offered or if it was Rhain who took, but it didn't matter, because the experience was sublime.

When their breathing settled, Rhain sat up and started tossing small twigs into the pond. The man was beautiful in the muted sunlight, surrounded by green. "Our hour is almost up, I suppose. Should we do your laundry before we must give up this oasis?"

He sat up laughing. "Oh, my dear. I don't do my own laundry; that's why I have a crew. I'm too busy and much too important for that type of labor."

Rhain pushed him back onto the soft moss and covered him. "Too important or too arrogant?" He cocked one brow, and they laughed and then kissed until voices could be heard not far off. They dressed, collected their things, and walked to the shore.

Alastair already missed their solitude.

Lydia sat in the shade with her newly cleaned clothing strewn around, drying on scrubby bushes. Dunn kept an eye on her from where he stood, marking things off on a supply list. Tim was off somewhere, likely foraging for fruits and nuts.

Some men were still swimming, and the dinghies slipped back and forth to the ship with fresh supplies.

"We will eat well tonight and for the next couple of days. This area has berries, fruit, mushrooms, and other things to fill your belly. And if the hunting party does their job well, we will have game to roast." He heard Rhain's stomach rumble, and he gave the man a smile. "You certainly do have a healthy appetite. I guess that is how you grew so large."

In an unusual show of mischief, Rhain wiggled his eyebrows. "Actually, my appetite has increased immensely since I met you."

He squeezed Rhain's hand briefly. "Come, let's put your and Miss Lydia's clothing in the next boat going to the ship. One of my men will string them up to dry in your berths."

* * * *

It wasn't much later that Rhain realized all his tasks were complete, so he sat on a log with Lydia and listened to her wax poetic on how their piece of land would be just like this spot, if not even more lovely. How there would be a cove where their pirates could anchor their ship and come for a visit every few months.

The girl's ideas were quite ridiculous, as the *Hurricane* had a route to maintain and it took them a year to travel the whole course, and he wasn't at all certain their land abutted the ocean. However, he let her talk and just soaked up the happy feelings.

He must have nodded off at some point because his head jerked up painfully at Lydia's, "I must tell you something, Rhain, but only if you promise not to become angry."

"Well, that certainly got my attention, Lyd. Who did what, and how many people must I kill?"

She slapped his arm. "Oh, don't be silly. I am quite serious. Promise."

"I am more than quite serious, Lydia. Is it First Mate Conall Dunn? I certainly hope not; even though he is small, I do believe he will be rather difficult to dispatch."

Lydia laughed. The sound, clear and dry, was so endearing to Rhain, he wanted to cry for joy.

"No, Conall has been a perfect gentleman. Although I do very much care for him and wouldn't mind if he would let the chivalry go for a while now and again."

"Lydia," he growled, ready to interrogate her on the use of the man's first name.

She leaned closer. "What I want to tell you is that I have been kissed."

He shot up from the log and glared at the crowd of seamen on the sand. "Who? Tell me. That is totally inappropriate, and I will handle this straight away."

"Sit down, Rhain, or I'll tell you nothing more."

He sat, heart beating out in staccato rage, and scanned the crowd. No one looked their way. No one looked guilty. Damn and damn!

"It all happened so innocently, to be honest. I was sitting with Tim, drying off in the sun. I felt so wonderful after my bath that I started talking to her and admitted I didn't realize there were women who, like you, lusted after their own sex."

Rhain bridled and sought the female sailor in question. The woman worked alongside the men, pulling her own weight as if she had been born a man. She did not look like a Lydia-kissing tyrant.

"Anyway, I've always understood your attraction to men because, well, men are so desirable. I never realized it worked both ways. So I asked her to tell me why she would dally with women, and the things she told me…" Lydia fanned her face with one slim hand. "Dear me. And then I confessed I'd never been kissed. That I'd quite like it if Conall would kiss me—"

"Lydia!"

"Calm, brother. He hasn't even attempted, but I can have fantasies. I am one and twenty after all."

He frowned at that, not at all certain if he could demand his little sister to stop having fantasies.

"As I was saying, I confessed to her that I did not want to do a bad job of kissing if Conall actually did manage to do the deed with me. And I asked her to teach me."

"Lydia Morgan, of all the ridiculous ideas. How could you even come up with that…that, well, ridiculous idea?"

Lydia laughed.

Of all things.

"Don't be angry; you promised."

"No, actually, I didn't."

She continued as if it were a forgone conclusion that he would hold his temper.

Rhain was not as convinced.

"So she showed me. Showed me how to tilt my head to move our noses out of the way, how to relax my lips so the kiss didn't feel like a hard apple but like a soft apricot, how to open my mouth to let her tongue—"

Unable to sit still, he jumped up again. The image of Lydia with someone's tongue in her mouth set his stomach churning as if he'd eaten week-old stew. He could take this no longer. Pacing around their little private bit of sand, the sand stinging the bottom of his feet, he took one deep breath after another.

How could his sister, his precious little sister, be so bold? When had she even gotten old enough to want a tongue in her— No. He would not think about that. How had she matured without his notice and want a kiss from anyone? That thought was marginally less awful.

It seemed like a week ago she was a gangly child. Now she was kissing, not anyone mind you, but the only woman, who happened to be a deviant, on the ship.

Well, perhaps that was better than her kissing a man. After all, how much trouble could she manage with another woman? Yes, actually, that thought calmed him considerably, so he sat back down and let Lydia finish what she needed to tell him.

"May I continue?"

He snorted. "Oh, please do. I'm dying to learn what you got up to next."

Patting his arm, she continued. "So without going into any more details, she taught me how to kiss, and now I am comfortable that I will not embarrass myself if anyone ever invites me to do so."

"Lovely," he said, but the word came out sounding as if he'd just eaten an underripe plum.

They were quiet for a long while before he said, "Lyd, do you like women?"

She tilted her head. "I will have to think about this. As I never knew it was an option, I never considered it. I must admit I enjoyed the kisses. Tim is a good person, and her kisses were soft and she smelled sweet and fresh. I had these little tinglings in my belly." She fluttered a hand over her middle. "But I am certain I must kiss a man for comparison."

He sank his head into his hands. His sister would be the death of him.

"Don't fret, Rhain. You would not want me to make a decision without doing the proper research, would you?"

He shook his head in frustration, which she obviously took as encouragement.

"Of course. You're a man of intellect; you probably did the same thing, didn't you?"

In fact, he had, purchasing time with a whore, and then later tried again with Sally Blount, a pretty young seamstress who earned a bit extra now and again selling kisses and more. It did not work well for him for some reason; what was sought after by most healthy men made him anxious and was only mildly pleasant.

How could he chastise his sister for waiting years longer than he to do the same experimentation? He shook his head again.

"As I expected."

Apparently, she would read into his actions what she intended, so he was determined to sit and listen until she ran out of outrageous things to say.

"I plan to ask Conall tonight. After he drinks some rum. I think he will say yes."

"Lydia, this is a very dangerous idea. What if he can't restrain himself? What if he— "

"He won't, but in case he does, you will not be far away. I plan to stage this experience while you are near. Tonight, during the feast, I will lead him to the shadows, just there. Station yourself there." She pointed to a shadowed clearing, then to a flat boulder in the sand. "If I'm not out of the shadows in three…no, make that five minutes, come and rescue me from the clutches of a dastardly pirate." Her eyes glowed with humor, and her smile held so much lust for life that he, the stupid romantic, could not say no.

"I truly believe this is a stupid idea. Is there anything I can do to dissuade you?"

She shook her head, sprightly, near-white curls bobbing around her face.

He sighed, stood, and started to walk away. "What did I do to deserve you, sister?"

She laughed with all the enthusiasm of a drunken courtesan and called to his retreating back, "Imagine how much trouble I'd be if I'd been healthy these last few years."

He shivered at the thought.

* * * *

Rhain sat hunched over his tankard of rum punch, watching the spitted venison roast over hot coals, thinking about Lydia. He'd done her bidding. He'd spent the longest five minutes of his life while she disappeared into the dark with her sailor. In that time, he thought of at least a hundred ways to dispatch the reprobate, but when the two walked out from the shadows, Lydia's hand resting gently on the man's arm, it seemed so normal, so harmless, he didn't know what to do.

So he sat, drinking too much rum, and watched the seamen turn more and more rowdy.

Alastair sat beside him and handed him a plate. "That meat will take some time to cook. I thought we should start with the rest of the meal so we can row back to ship while the moon is still up."

Rhain noticed First Mate Dunn brought a plate to Lydia as well. The man acted like a proper courtier and not like the man who had just kissed his sister in the damn bushes. He ate the stewed bitter greens, wild onions, and mushrooms. They tasted excellent, even in his foul mood.

Dessert was a mixture of unidentifiable plum-sized, purple fruit and tart berries drizzled with honey. A rare treat for this group, he assumed, so he forced back worry long enough to express his enjoyment and thanks.

The good food and rum released his tension. As the sun slipped below the trees, the near deafening sound of birds shifted to the sound of nocturnal insects. The island noises were startling after the monotonous sound of the sea for so many weeks.

Making certain to keep Lydia within sight, he began to enjoy himself again. The ocean's surface glistened, reflecting the sky's lavender and navy hues. He enjoyed the heat of Alastair sitting next to him. He could become used to this closeness, the uninhibited relationship. In fact, he'd acclimated to parts of it already and knew he would sorely miss the gorgeous pirate when they disembarked on Dominica. He was suddenly very sad. Most likely due to the two measures of rum he'd been given.

Alastair talked amicably about trivial matters. "There were three deer in all. Two will be consumed tonight; the other will serve as stew stock for the next few days. About a dozen fowl will fill in the rest of the meals with meat. Everyone should be well fed and satisfied until we reach Dominica, this being the last stop, barring unforeseen issues."

A light touch on his leg brought his full attention to Alastair. "What has you troubled?"

He nodded at the first mate laughing with Lydia.

"Ah, I see. Not to worry, Mate Dunn is an honorable man. He will do nothing Miss Lydia does not fully agree to."

"What about my wishes in the matter?"

"Well, I imagine your sister will consider those, but Mate Dunn will likely not concern himself with your wishes as long as Miss Lydia knows her own mind."

Rhain spluttered. "But I'm her brother, her guardian."

"Um, yes, but out here rules are different. She can decide for herself."

And there was the rub. Lydia, as strong-willed as ever, had the right to make her own decisions, unless he acted as a dictator. Which might not be a bad thing under the circumstances.

Alastair, apparently unconcerned about the unfolding drama, said, "We will sleep on board. It is safer there, and some of the crew will stay aboard anyway to keep things running smoothly. We'll leave before the moon sets so we can see to row to ship."

Eventually the venison was served as the moon crept over their watery cove. They would need to leave soon because the men were getting rum happy.

A handful of the crew sang bawdy ballads, and about twelve men danced uncoordinated jigs with elbows and knees poking this way and that. A wrestling match enticed men to yelling and making bets, and there were occasional shoves and angry curses.

Rhain sank his teeth into tough but flavorful meat, one side crispy, the other juicy. "Mhh. Good."

"I agree," Alastair said as he tore off another bite with strong white teeth.

When he finished the meat and licked his fingers clean, Rhain used a tiny stick to pick venison fibers from between his front teeth.

Alastair said, "Time to go to the ship before those clouds"—he pointed out over the water—"obscure the moon. Let's round up your sister. Mate Dunn will stay here with the crew to keep order."

The increasing rowdiness of the crew was worrisome. "Can't you keep them under control?"

Alastair shrugged. "They need a release and a chance to work their frustrations out now and again. There will be a few fights, a few bouts of sick stomachs tomorrow, but they all know if they are not lifting and hefting their share in the morning, they will not sail with us. Usually everything works out fine."

"And when it doesn't?"

"When it doesn't... Well, I don't much like those days." Alastair picked up his plate and tin cup, neatly avoiding the question. "Come along, it's back to the ship for us."

"Just a moment. I'll, umm, visit the bushes to relieve myself of some of this fine rum."

Alastair laughed and offered to help, but Rhain declined adamantly.

Rhain enjoyed his nice rum euphoria that was enhanced by the incredible surroundings of a wild and beautiful paradise.

He staggered when entering the privacy of the scrub bushes and opened his falls. Something moved in the forest a few yards away. He called out, "Hello. You didn't miss out on the feast, did you? Go down and grab some, then. No time to waste."

No reply.

He finished his necessaries, buttoned up, and turned.

Something flashed in the moonlight.

He shifted as a large staff swung toward his head, missed, and hit his shoulder. Ducking, he reached up and grabbed for the staff, but it swung again.

This time he ducked and lunged at the attacker's legs.

The man stumbled back, fell, and Rhain was on him, giving him a face and gut full of fists.

Curling into a ball, the miscreant avoided all but a few of Rhain's punches. Then, in a show of strength, the large man under him planted his feet, bucked his hips, and wrestled Rhain off.

Rhain righted himself and reached for the man, but he was already running into the forest.

Rhain sat up, rubbing sweat from his eyes. What the hell had that been about?

Staggering with the first few steps he took, he slowly and cautiously made his way back to the beach. Sighting Alastair, he relaxed, realizing that for the first time in a very long time, he would not have to deal with this alone.

* * * *

"There are three of them," Dunn whispered after letting the men go back to work.

"Which three?" Alastair spat the words with a hatred he had not felt in years. Squinting from the early morning sun, he perused his men, looking for the telltale signs of a fight.

After Rhain told him what happened, they took the last boat to the ship. They'd not made love last night; instead, they held each other as if the threat of harm to Rhain gave them both a need for simple comfort.

First thing that morning, they scouted their men to see if any sported new bruises or cuts. Dunn did most of the scrutinizing, while Alastair continued to organize the land parties.

"One-armed Sam…" Who actually possessed two perfectly fit arms. "Teko, but he is too small to fit Mr. Morgan's description of the attacker, and… You're not going to like this."

He glared at Dunn. "Tell me."

"Balls."

"Damnation."

"My thoughts exactly. That man has been a thorn in my side ever since you started sleeping with him."

"Now that is not at all fair."

"No?"

"No, I only slept with him for a month. After I broke it off, he should have stopped acting like he deserved special treatment."

"Well, he hasn't. I'm certain he still thinks he can convince you to take him back. That tiny head of his probably thinks if he gets rid of Mr. Morgan, he will be in your bed the next night. And if he gets into your bed, eventually he will convince you he is a better man for the first-mate post."

"We don't know that; you're speculating."

"Doesn't matter; we need rid of him anyway. Let's leave him here."

"But what if it was Sam? We can't assume we have gotten rid of the problem and then have something else happen. Especially at sea."

"Leave them both."

Shaking his head, he said, "That would be inhumane. It is a good ten miles to the nearest port with nothing in between." He turned to look at the woods and waved a hand. "This island might be teeming with savages or large predators. We don't know; we never venture far from this spot when we come here."

"Lock them both up until we dock in Dominica. It will only be two days, at any rate."

"No, if they are left on Dominica, that is too close to Mr. Morgan and Miss Lydia. Besides, one of the men is innocent."

"What, then?"

"I will talk with Mr. Morgan. Maybe he's quarreled with one of the men. That might uncover the culprit."

Dunn nodded and went on about his duty.

Two days.

Two days and Rhain would be out of his life. Possibly forever. Damn, but that man slipped under his skin without notice. He wanted to keep him, protect him, sleep with him curled up beside him every night.

How did I let this happen? He knew the man would be leaving once they reached Dominica. But the affection between them crept up on him until one day it was just there. A permanent part of him now. The threat to Rhain's safety, his life, forced him to admit his feelings at least to himself.

He found Rhain sitting with Miss Lydia and interrupted their quiet conversation. They both jerked their gazes to him, eyes round, and Miss Lydia's mouth in a guilty-looking *O*.

What the devil was that all about?

"A word with you, Mr. Morgan?"

"Of course." He smiled at his sister. "I'll be right back, love."

They walked along the beach away from the crowd, Rhain unbearably handsome with a faint smile on his lips. "We have identified two men that may have attacked you last night. They are both large and very strong, so it could be either. Have you had any other confrontations on ship that would let us identify the culprit?"

"There were any number of glares and mutters, but nothing more than that. Honestly, I paid little attention."

"Would you recognize any of the men showing disrespect?"

"Perhaps one or two of them, but not all, of that I'm certain."

"There is a man just left of the closest skiff. Take a good look at him. Do you recognize him as one of the men glaring at you?"

Rhain considered the man for a long time and from various angles as Sam moved barrels of water into the small boat. Rhain shook his head. "No, actually, I don't believe I've been in that man's company much. Would be hard to ignore him, what with that shock of red hair."

Alastair agreed. Sam would be difficult to miss in a crowd. "And that man over there, sitting on the rock pretending to fix a rope?" Balls was busy watching everything that went on but accomplishing next to nothing. Why hadn't he noticed this about the man? Before, all he saw was someone big and strong who could wind up his desire and push it over the edge.

No. For a time, he'd ignored the man's complaints and willingness to stir up trouble. After the affair, the thought to rid himself of the man crossed his mind a few times, but that felt retaliatory, and he let the man stay on.

Rhain did not even have to think about it. "Yes, he definitely does not seem to like my presence on ship. I've seen more than a few glimpses of malice from that one. What did I do to garner his dislike?"

"Balls and I—"

"Balls?" Rhain chuckled.

"Yes, Balls, not called that for any unusual anatomical formations, mind you, but for his fierceness in battle." He looked at Rhain, admiring his size and bulk. "I'd say you were lucky to sustain no damage, but I'm thankful that you did not."

"I do quite enjoy the more brutal sports. Turns out my training helped in a real fight." He looked at Balls. "And the reason he dislikes me?"

Alastair cleared his throat. "Yes, about that... I broke a very important rule."

"What rule?"

"I fucked a crew member."

Rhain spun on his heel and strode down the beach again.

Alastair followed.

"Balls. You fucked Balls?"

"Yes." Why did he feel he must explain his actions? He was a healthy man in his prime; no one would expect him to be celibate. He explained nonetheless. "It ended a few months ago. I ended it, rather. The man was more interested than I, said he wanted to be my matelot— my long-term, committed lover. It started to cause problems between us and with other members of the crew, so I ended the affair. I thought he'd accepted our liaison was over. Apparently, he did not.

"Rhain, stop rushing so that we may discuss this civilly."

Rhain looked over his shoulder, a flush on his cheeks, and then looked forward, his tread barely slowing.

"So what will you do now? Your last lover doesn't like your current lover. I suppose that is only natural under the circumstances."

"I thought I might chain him belowdecks. After all, it is only two days until we reach Dominica and you are safely on land."

Rhain stopped dead in his tracks. "Two days?"

"Yes, why?"

"I…I didn't realize."

He touched Rhain's shoulder. "Is everything all right? What is troubling you?"

Shaking off Alastair's touch, Rhain continued walking. "I suppose when I'm gone, you will let him out. Will let him…"

"No, Rhain. That ship sailed months ago. I no longer want that man, whether you are here or not." He reached out, but then let his arm fall. "Do you believe me?"

"Yes, actually I do. It's just that I have much to think about right now. I heard some disturbing information from Lydia as well. Probably something I should tell you."

"Go ahead." Was Miss Lydia's illness returning? That was certainly bad news; she'd seemed so healthy the past weeks.

"It seems she has started experimenting with kisses."

"Kisses?"

"Indeed. She started practicing with Tim—"

"What?" He spluttered the response.

"Quiet! And then moved on to your first mate."

"Of all the bloody… Nothing more than kissing?"

"Thank God, not yet. It probably is a good thing we will be leaving this ship…in two days."

Alastair's mood sank to the bottom of the sea. That was probably true; otherwise, Alastair's heart would become irrevocably entangled with this irresistible man.

"So, which kiss did she like the best?"

Laughing, Rhain said, "She quite liked them both but said the butterflies in her stomach after Conall's kiss were large and numerous. Her words, not mine."

He gave Rhain credit for finding humor in the situation.

"I'm afraid I will spend the rest of my days keeping her out of trouble."

"That may well be your fate. Miss Lydia certainly does have a lust for life."

"Yes." He smiled. "So good to see after years of worrying if she would wake to see the next day."

They ran out of beach, and both seemed unable to face abandoning their time together. Pointing to a large piece of driftwood nestled under a tree, Alastair led Rhain there, and they sat watching the aqua-blue water rippling. His crew went about their duties, calling to one another, and the faint clatter of their chores carried on the humid breeze.

Rhain laced his fingers through Alastair's, the touch so bittersweet, his heart lurched a few times in his chest.

"I worry about her. I do believe she has developed tender feelings for First Mate Dunn. How will she manage after the two of you sail away?" He did not look at Alastair as he spoke.

Was this comment about Lydia or about Rhain himself? Alastair squeezed his fingers but had no idea what to say.

"Care for a swim? Race you to the water," Rhain said as he launched himself up. He stripped off his shirt and ran for the water before Alastair had a chance to react.

"Not fair. You gave no warning." He laughed and slowed his pace to watch the firm, pale arse and thighs of his lover before he dived into the rippling water.

They left paradise at midday.

* * * *

It was a rare treat to sleep in fresh linens that were not gritty with salt caked into each and every fiber. So Rhain retired to his berth for some time alone. He undressed, lay on the bunk, and enjoyed the island smells trapped in the bedding.

"Ahh." He'd barely closed his eyes and relaxed his muscles when a knock sounded on his flimsy door.

He sighed, then grumbled, "Never any peace on this damn boat." He resigned himself to losing his few minutes of solitude and slipped on some trousers.

The moment he opened the door and saw the captain lounging against the opposite wall, he no longer cared to be alone.

"It is a ship, not a boat."

He grabbed the lithe man by the belt and pulled him into the tiny space.

Alastair was bare-chested in seconds, and they were kissing with a fierceness that belied their encounter in the captain's cabin a mere hour before.

"Quick. This must be quick. I've something to show you."

"I have something to show you too," Rhain announced, as he stripped out of his trousers and drawers.

Alastair laughed. Stripping his trousers off, he lay naked on the bunk. "Yes, that thick cock is worth missing many things for, but this is something I think you will regret not seeing if we don't hurry."

"I'm good with a fast toss-off. Are you?"

"Even better would be a fast suck-off. Lie on top of me, with your face at my rod."

Just the thought of this act, which Rhain never considered before, set him to near exploding. Oh, yes. He would definitely enjoy this new fast suck-off.

Positioning himself in the most erotic tangle of body and limbs of his life, he felt wet heat surround his length before he even had a chance to enjoy the prettiness of his lover's cock. "God. That feels... Oh, God. So good." He engulfed the staff with much less finesse than he planned and shot his load down his pirate's throat before he even elicited a groan from the man.

It took several moments before he gained the control needed to caress and nuzzle competently enough to have his lover bucking and moaning. A few moments after that and he held the musky taste of Alastair's come in his mouth.

Then he was smacked on the arse and unceremoniously dumped onto the floor.

"What the—"

"Up. Dress. You must see this." Alastair dressed in a flash. How he managed to do that in such a small space, Rhain would never know.

"What the deuces is so important to see that you deprive me of my post-climax cuddle?"

Alastair threw Rhain's trousers, and they hit him in the face. "Shut up, dress, and come to the main deck, and you will find out." The man was out the door before Rhain even managed to pull up his drawers.

"Damn pirate. What the bloody hell has gotten into you?" But Rhain was the only one who heard his complaint, as the captain was already topside.

GOD, HE COULD not stop staring. The expression of awe on Rhain's face was breathtaking. The dolphins gave a good show as they sailed west, escorting them away from the island. Jumping and chittering with occasional backflips. They were one of the best parts of sailing. Always lifting the spirits of the crew. Making everyone laugh. Alastair wished he could talk to them and ask why they were always so jolly.

The show was over all too soon. After a handful of minutes, the merry group swam away, after a school of fish, he presumed.

"That..." Rhain cleared his throat. "That was one of the most incredible things I've ever seen."

"Yes. I thought it would be. Next time I tell you to move your arse, be quick about it."

Rhain smiled. "It was amazing to see. Thank you. However, what we did belowdeck was one of the most amazing things I've ever experienced. So I don't feel deprived by only seeing the animals for a few minutes. They were marvelous, but you were more so."

The sensation in his body at that moment had to be akin to how a glow worm felt when it lit its body to attract a mate. He didn't know it was possible to feel this whole, this complete, and this wonderful.

Lydia rushed over. "Rhain, did you see the huge gray fish that leapt in and out of the water? Oh, I forget what they are called."

"Dolphins. Playful creatures. And friendly as well."

Lydia squeezed Rhain's arm. "They look so intelligent."

"They are," added Alastair. "There are many stories about them saving shipwrecked seamen."

"Oh, how grand." She clapped her hands. "I'm going to find Tim to see if she knows any of those stories." Lydia rushed away, as fast as a ray of sun doused by a cloud.

The dolphins no longer followed the ship, but Alastair loitered with Rhain at the bulwarks. There was little to do at the moment but maintain course, which Dunn executed to perfection.

Alastair enjoyed spending the day with his lover, one of the few they had remaining together, watching waves slap the bow and later watching foam form and float away from the ship's stern as they sailed at eight knots and sliced through aqua water.

Even better was watching the breeze ruffle hair that was no longer short and tidy. The brown hair was unruly, tempting. He wanted nothing more than to grab those curls and pull Rhain in for a searing kiss.

Instead, he acted the gentleman, and they talked about inconsequential things. Occasionally, Lydia would stop by to chat and then go off to find something more entertaining.

So engrossed in his companion, he was surprised not to notice the growing humidity, still air, and clouds building, until his second in command pointed them out. Usually he felt humidity like a sixth sense. It wrapped around him like an old shirt when it promised good winds and smothered like a burlap scarf wrapped about his head when too high and threatening a storm.

This felt like two burlap scarfs, an earlier sign than the clouds, which were just a smudge on the horizon. Less blue, more gray than the rest of the sky, like all color had leached from the heavens.

"Trouble?"

"Could be. Too early to tell. Better start getting the ship ready just in case. These storms can move in faster than you would expect." He left to start giving orders.

His crew worked seamlessly together, having done this drill many times before. So when the humidity rose to unbearable levels and the direction of the wind changed, the little ship was ready.

Lydia and Rhain were at the bulwark together.

Alastair took a deep breath and walked over to prepare them. "Here is where we stand. We are too far away from any of the islands to make it to a safe anchorage before this storm reaches us. The cloud bank is immense; no hope we can go around. We've readied the ship and will ride this squall out. Please don't worry; we have done this many times. However, there are things you need to do to keep yourselves safe.

"We've turned the ship into the teeth of the wind. That way the waves will hit the bow straight on. However, the ship will bounce and jerk as the waves come at us. Some may be large and can shift direction quickly."

Lydia's blue eyes grew big as soup spoons, and Rhain said, "What you mean is, we will bounce around like a cork in a cook pot, don't you?"

He sighed but would not prevaricate. They needed to know the truth of this situation. "I need you both in your berths with the lee cloth engaged and all your belongings stowed and secured. I would hate for either of you to be hurt because you or something in your room gets flung about."

"Can we not stay in your quarters?" Rhain asked. "I don't think I will like being bounced around that minuscule berth."

Alastair shook his head. "Your rooms are below the captain's cabin and will be more stable and safer."

Rhain's complexion went white. "And where will you be?"

"Steering the ship, of course." He smiled.

"Up there?" Rhain pointed to the wheel. "Where you will be exposed like a dried bone poking through skin? On the topmost deck?" His face now almost ashen.

"Quiet your fears, now. I will not be defenseless. I will be strapped on, and I've done this many times. It is quite exhilarating and addictive, to be honest. After your first storm, you start looking forward to more."

Miss Lydia's brow wrinkled, but she gave him a wide smile, grabbing Rhain's arm. "As much as I'd like to witness the storm, I think it would be best if we tuck ourselves in, don't you, brother?" She pulled the man's arm, and he reluctantly followed. "Best of luck, Captain. Take us to Dominica safely."

He tapped his forehead. "Yes, Mama."

Rhain broke away from her grip and kissed Alastair soundly. "Do be careful." And then they were gone, and Alastair had this feeling in his chest that gave him a surge of invincibility.

* * * *

Two hours later, Rhain lay strapped in his bunk with lee cloths, hat in one hand, death grip on the wooden bed frame with the other.

The ship took another dive, then crashed and lifted rapidly. He moaned.

Lydia called from her adjacent room. "Are you unwell, dear? Do you need me to come help you?"

"No. Stay where you are. I just have a small stomach ailment. I'll be—"

The ship lurched again, water sloshing about on the floor, and he lost his lunch directly into his hat. Damnation, he had never been so goddamn miserable in his life. How much longer would the accursed storm last?

Lydia must have heard him, for she started talking. Actually, she must have been yelling to be heard over the thunder and groans of the ship. She talked about their island, and what their house would look like, and if their neighbors would invite them to a welcoming dinner.

She must have kept this up, to keep his mind off the storm, for about an hour, when his door opened and Alastair stumbled in as the ship jolted. He dripped water, black hair slicked to his head and cheeks, but he smiled.

"Mate Dunn relieved me for a time, so I thought I'd check on my two favorite passengers."

They were his only passengers, but Rhain felt too awful to state the obvious.

"How are you, Miss Lydia?" he yelled.

"Quite well, Captain. Thank you for looking in on us. I do believe my brother could use your assistance."

And Alastair did assist. He made the befouled hat disappear, and Rhain hoped he never saw the thing again.

Alastair returned with wet and dry toweling and offered the best balm to Rhain's shattered nerves and roiling stomach. "The waves have started to settle, and we can see sun off to the southeast. This is a huge gale, but she barely clipped us. It will be over soon."

Rhain would have cheered if he weren't afraid that would cause him to cast up his accounts in front of the man he spent time naked with. He settled for a weak smile instead.

Running a light, wet cloth across Rhain's face, Alastair said, "In a few moments I think we can unstrap you, but I don't want you to sit up fast. That will make your stomach worse." The man started working on the restraint.

"Now, sit slowly, and keep your eyes open."

He did as bid, and once his head elevated above his stomach, he felt immediately better. "Ah, this is good. I think I might live."

Alastair laughed, kissed his forehead, and left to check on Lydia.

Half an hour later, cleaned, refreshed, and almost fully recovered, he stumbled topside on shaky limbs with Lydia leading the way. They watched the storm receding. The distant lightning and thunder were incredible to witness once the ship stopped bouncing like a spirited horse with its first rider.

Sailors dashed about tying sails and securing ropes. Water still pooled in unusual places.

First Mate Dunn sought them out. "I have some small bad news, I'm afraid."

His stomach sank as if the ship were falling into a wave's trench. "What is that?"

"Even though we have made very good time thus far, the storm forced us off course, and we need to make a few repairs; our docking in Dominica will be delayed by another few days." The man smiled and squeezed Lydia's hand as he said this.

Lydia bounced on her toes and exclaimed, "We have an extra few days? We have the rest of today and two others? That is a boon, not bad news. Wonderful news!"

Rhain caught the captain's eye, who once again manned the wheel, and could feel his face stretch into an almost painfully large smile.

* * * *

Rhain rubbed his full belly. "I very much appreciate that last provisioning stop. I don't believe we ever ate this well in London."

Hugging his arm close to her thin side, Lydia said, "That berry dessert was wonderful, I must agree."

They walked slowly arm in arm around the ship, while Alastair and First Mate Dunn carried out some ship business. Afterward, Rhain planned to spend the night keeping his captain awake and occupied with a more sensual business.

"Oh, just look at all those stars. There must be hundreds of thousands of them. Hard to believe that just a day ago this sky was full of storm clouds."

Hushed voices behind a group of secured crates ruined the feeling of isolation. Damn, but there was no privacy on ship. The whispering, and the sound of feet rapidly slapping on wood demanded his full attention.

Men—two, three, perhaps more—rushed around the crates and headed directly toward them.

Heart pounding, he reacted before verifying the intention of those men. He shoved Lydia behind him and made himself as large as possible. There would be no way those men would pass him and accost his sister.

He vaguely registered Lydia crying for help as the first man reached him. Rhain dispatched the man quickly by blocking the swing of a long board, stepping inside the swing, and punching the man in the throat. The man was yet to slip fully to the deck when the next man swung a short pole, striking Rhain in the thigh. It was a weak swing at an awkward angle.

He could have taken this man down as well if not for the third man tossing a coil of rope at his head. He dodged and went for the second man again just as he saw Alastair out of the corner of his eye. The captain jumped from the quarterdeck, landing two feet away from the third man, snapped his neck as smooth as you please, and was facing a fourth man before the dead man slumped to the main deck.

Rhain had yet to count the fourth man among the miscreants. It was Balls, and the man looked crazed with anger.

Dunn ran past him as the second man tried for another swing. This time, Rhain stepped toward the swing, hitting the man's forearm, which broke the swing's momentum. He grabbed the man's arm and pulled him and his ugly face into a left hook. Not even looking to see if the man was still alive or fighting, he turned to find Lydia. She was safely behind Dunn, who smoothly pulled a knife out of the first man's neck and hauled the body overboard.

He pivoted. The second man lay still, but Balls was the threat now.

Alastair, behind Balls, had a short staff pulled tight against the struggling giant's neck. "How did you scramble your sorry arse out of irons, you waste of skin?"

Balls only gurgled and struggled more violently.

Rhain stepped up and punched the thug in the nose. The man went down, and Alastair and Rhain followed him, pulling his arms up behind his back, not giving him a chance to regain his senses.

Dunn was there with a length of rope before either of them could call for it, and tied the big man up tight roughly.

Only then did Rhain realize a large part of the crew was milling around trying to determine what happened and offering help.

Alastair looked at Rhain, holding his gaze as he caught his breath. "I thought…" He swallowed. "Never mind. What happened?"

Filling the captain and Dunn in on the little he knew, he was relieved when Lydia came over and leaned against him. He didn't even have to ask; Lydia offered a, "I am fine, Rhain. Conall dispatched the man before he regained his strength after your superlative punch. Bravo, brother. And you, Captain, what an artist you are at fighting. Perhaps you will teach me how to use my knife?" Then she was off to fuss over Dunn, and Rhain took that moment to feel the crippling fear he should have felt moments ago.

His body shook, his hands cold as the north wind. "God, Alastair. God, I thought Lydia, and…and then I thought you were going to…" He put his head in his hands, and Alastair wrapped him in a warm embrace, murmuring meaningless phrases.

Feeling like a child, he collected his composure and pushed away from his lover. "Thank you."

Alastair only smiled. "Your sister was correct; nice punches, Rhain. Perhaps you can teach me some of your techniques."

"From what I was able to see, you don't need any additional techniques. You are a lethal man." Just as he had suspected that first day in the Red Pig.

"What will you do to him?" He nodded toward Balls, who was starting to struggle against his restraints.

"Talk to him, and that one."

The second man was still out cold.

"See how they got Balls out of lockup, find out if anyone else was involved, and force them to tell me what they hoped to gain from this attack. My suspicion is they thought they could garner enough help to take over the ship." He snorted.

Rhain also doubted they would have been successful. The crew— most of it, at any rate—were unusually loyal to the captain.

Lydia came over to them. "Don't kill them."

"Why not?" Alastair said as if her comment were farcical.

"It is not conscionable to kill someone when they are tied up and helpless."

Alastair looked at Rhain and winked. He stood. "Smith, Lefty, and Cook, throw these two men belowdeck, and two of you stand guard at all times. Don't allow them to talk to one another.

"Mr. Morgan, Miss Lydia, Mate Dunn, care for a spot of port to wash the taste of danger from our mouths?"

They all nodded.

Chapter Ten

Their last evening on the *Hurricane*, Rhain sat with Lydia, watching the setting sun play over straggling orange-and-purple tinged clouds. It was lovely, but both he and his sister sat quietly, Lydia almost scowling, and he knew his expression must be similarly morbid.

She sighed. "I must be honest. I don't want to leave the ship."

He patted her pale hand.

"I've never been so happy as on this ship. I feel well, almost as though I never was ill. And…promise you will not anger?"

"Lydia, do stop saying that! It has the opposite effect of what you're asking for."

"Promise."

"No."

"I have fallen in love."

Rhain snorted. "That is not news, Lyd. You walk around in a cloud of joy and stare like a puppy at First Mate Dunn all day long."

She smiled at that. "So you see why I want to stay."

He nodded, letting her talk, knowing her wish was impossible for both of them. But he enjoyed the fantasy for a few wonderful moments.

Clasping his closest hand, she enthused, "We could both stay. I know you're in love with your captain."

He snorted, a cocktail of emotions running through him. Lust, certainly. Friendship, yes. Love by the slop bucketfuls, but what good was that emotion when he was getting ready to leave ship? Oh, God. It would hurt to leave one hundred times more than when Robert left him.

"I'm certain Captain Breckenridge will let us stay. I've become quite good at splicing rope and educating the crew on what they want to learn. I can continue keeping his books, and you are proving to be a quick study at navigation. I'm certain you would be excellent at that."

"No, Lydia."

She continued as if he had not spoken, and he felt his anger grow. He was angry because she spun a tale that sounded so perfect, and it was within their reach, but they couldn't. It would be disastrous.

He and Alastair would eventually fight, since they were both rather hotheaded, and he'd likely find himself tossed off ship someplace overrun with flesh-eating insects the size of his fist. Lydia would marry much below her station, find herself with child and then dumped at a port town where she would see Dunn every other year. Probably getting a new round of pregnancy with each short visit.

The first mate came toward them, so he stopped Lydia's dream weaving. "No. We have a plantation that needs our input, and we must maintain our position in society. I'm sure you will find a nice wealthy second son of a governor, or some such, in Dominica, and will be happier than you can imagine with new gowns and hair ribbons."

She glared at him.

Dunn held out his arm for Lydia. "Miss Lydia, Mr. Morgan, the captain's dinner party is ready. Please allow me to escort you in."

He could admit the first mate did have tolerable manners for a lowborn, he thought as he followed him to the captain's chamber for what Alastair termed "a celebration dinner." Although celebrating *what*, he didn't know. One could have scooped up the melancholy in that room with a spoon, it was so thick.

Lydia glared at him every time their eyes met, and he had a sick stomach from the knowledge this was his last day on ship and didn't enjoy the food. Admittedly, the quality had somewhat dwindled that day since they'd run out of fresh meat.

Thankfully, the tense affair finished quickly, as no one lingered over wine or port. Dunn offered to walk Lydia around the main deck and then escort her to her berth.

"Still no word from your captives?" Rhain asked while Alastair locked the cabin door.

"Nothing, but I'm not concerned. They will talk when their gullet is so dry they can no longer swallow."

That thought made his own throat feel like parchment. He once again took his place at the table and swallowed another mouthful of port.

Alastair reached across the scared wood and laced their fingers together. His loose white shirt was open at the neck, offering a tempting glimpse of tan chest, but Rhain moved to kiss that skin because his lover looked as though he'd lost his entire crew in a game of cards.

Well, no time like the present. "Lydia says she is in love and wants to stay on ship." He laughed and rolled his eyes, expecting Alastair to do the same, but instead he squeezed their fingers tighter together.

"I would be quite angry with your first mate if it weren't that I know my sister is just as much to blame, perhaps more than he is."

Nodding, Alastair looked at their entwined hands, so Rhain studied them as well. One dark, long and elegant, the other light, freckled and large.

"She's always been fanciful, so don't concern yourself with such a ridiculous notion."

"I am not irritated, nor concerned." And indeed, the man looked anything but. He looked downtrodden.

"Yes, well… Not to worry, I told her that was unacceptable and that tomorrow, as soon as we docked, we would move to the plantation to start our new life."

Alastair looked up at that. "She could stay. You both could."

For one very brief moment, his heart filled his throat and he couldn't breathe. But then he stamped out the surge of elation, and unfortunately anger filled its place. "Oh, not you also. Is this whole ship filled with dreamers? And you, sir, are old enough to know better, whereas Lydia is still almost a child. I hope you were not filling her head with this nonsense. Or your first mate's head either."

Unable to sit any longer, he stood and then prowled around the small room.

He barely heard the next ridiculous thing Alastair said.

"Rhain, I have rarely cared for anyone. Damnation, I hardly even know my own family. But I have come to care for you. Both of you really, but you in particular." With his head bent, his long, unbound hair hiding his face, Alastair continued. "I find myself thinking of ways to delay arriving at Dominica."

At Rhain's gasp of surprise, he turned and continued, those black eyes staring directly at him. "Don't even think that. I did nothing to delay your trip, although I did fantasize about doing so." He stood and walked over, placing a hand on Rhain's chest. "You, my prickly bastard, I will miss greatly." And he leaned in for a light, tender kiss, his eyes closed.

Rhain watched emotions play over the handsome face before he himself got caught up in the kiss, deepening it. "God, Alastair." He mashed his hardening cock against his lover's already rock-hard member. "I want to fuck you so hard you won't be able to walk tomorrow." Actually, he needed to claim Alastair so utterly and completely the man would never forget him.

They stumbled to the bed, undoing each other's clothes. They were naked and writhing against each other in moments, kissing as if their survival depended on it. But Rhain wanted, *needed*, more. He slid down the lean muscled body, unfastening, unbuckling, and untying as he went, and took a good look at the fine long cock, wanting to taste it. He did.

He licked up the length and then wrapped his mouth around the silky-hard rod and sucked all the way to the base. His nose pressed in the crease of Alastair's groin, and he inhaled the fragrance so unique to this man.

How does one describe a scent if words cannot capture its essence? But he knew he would remember that smell, that taste, until the day he died. Would remember it, alone in his bed. While gray-haired and remorseful. Damn it all to hell.

Alastair moaned and pumped his hips, one hand in Rhain's hair pulling, hips pushing. A board on the bed groaned in protest.

It was going to end too soon, like this. He wanted more.

He pulled off and issued one of his own commands, "Turn over."

Alastair's eyes flew open at the harsh utterance, but he turned over. One knee caught Rhain in the gut, and it took a moment to straighten out arms and legs.

God, Alastair had a fine arse. His cock throbbed with a need for release as he ran his hands down the lean, firm cheeks. His fingers roamed into the tight recesses where the skin darkened. He placed his thumb on the puckering hole, and it constricted, then relaxed, just enough for the tip of his thumb to breach the surface.

He almost came then and grabbed his sac with a pinching twist to keep from spilling. He took a deep breath and was under control again. He pressed at Alastair's anus harder until his thumb slid all the way into that dry passage. In his need, he'd forgotten to prepare his lover with oil. Damn.

He spat, thought better of it, then bent down and kissed the entrance that he would conquer, would own.

Alastair groaned, "No," when Rhain removed his thumb, but started whimpering when Rhain pressed his lips and tongue in its place. He kissed and licked and pressed in as far as he could go, loving the way his lover writhed under him, the musky taste on his tongue. "I'm going to take that arse. I'm going to own it, and you will never ever forget who plowed you this night."

"Yes, Rhain. Now. Do it now."

He almost forgot the oil again in his lust-filled haze. But at the last moment he remembered, and then lunged across the room and had the oil back before he could exhale.

They made quick work of the preparation, not sure if it was his or Alastair's impatience as the man bucked back against his fingers just as Rhain pushed into the tight hole he longed to possess.

When he slipped into the puckered opening, watching Alastair's athletic body and lush hair skimming his shoulder blades and slipping down to brush the sheets, hiding that beloved face, Rhain nearly cried his joy and screamed his pain. The pain of knowing this was their last night.

He pounded into his beautiful captain. The man's arse cheeks flexed and relaxed with his own thrusts, his hair swaying in an intoxicating flow of ebony with each movement. But Rhain could not force his way close enough, nor deep enough.

He grabbed Alastair's shoulders and pulled him up against his own chest. The man groaned and almost melted as Rhain pummeled his sweet spot.

The creak of the wooden bed, the sound of balls slapping arse, and the pop of air compressing inside his lover combined in a vulgar enhancement to their lovemaking.

Alastair shot as he yelled, "I love you. Fuck. Love. Goddamn you. Don't... You can't... I love you."

The declaration, meaningless given the intensity of the fuck, forced his own climax nonetheless, and Rhain yelled answering curses of pleasure and anguish in his lover's hair. "Yes, come around my cock. Take my seed. Be my..."

Years of pent-up anger and fear rushed out with his seed, and he sobbed—just once—into Alastair's sweat-matted hair.

They sank to the mattress as their muscles fatigued. Rhain's prick slipped out as they collapsed, wrapped tightly in each other's arms.

Chapter Eleven

The next afternoon, Rhain draped a comforting arm around Lydia, who clutched a handkerchief, twisting the tortured cloth this way, then that. Occasionally the cloth was used to wipe angrily at her wet cheeks.

Breakfast had been a quiet affair as they tacked around the leeward side of Dominica. Alastair ate little and stared into his tea. Rhain, for some unforeseen reason, was ravenous and ate his share and more. Neither of them talked until it was time for Alastair to perform his captain's duties.

Dressed and looking finer than a five-tier cake, Alastair said, "We will have little privacy above deck, so I will say good-bye now." He held out a strong, elegant hand, and they shook, slowly. "I have enjoyed your company beyond imagining, and hope..." His voice broke. "We will see each other again soon. My dear, dear prickly bastard." He smiled a slow half smile and stepped gently into Rhain's embrace. "Be happy."

Rhain nodded, terribly close to tears.

And then Alastair was out the door, off to his myriad mysterious duties.

For an hour, he and Lydia stood watching Dominica grow on the horizon, neither mentioning that Dominica looked nothing like the paradise they'd envisioned for the past several months. The port town was flat for many miles until steep peaks shot up with pale lavender and brown streaks. Nothing was green. A dry yellow-brown that looked like mud engulfed the majority of the island. A disturbing, ugly haze blanketed the town all the way to the slopes of the mountains.

Surely, they would not live close to this town. The air in London would be considered clean compared to that of this humid, stewing, smoke-clogged location.

"Rhain? I am somewhat worried about this."

Truth be told, he was as well and could do nothing but squeeze her shoulder. "Don't worry, dear. Our plantation will be miles away from this...place."

Lydia sobbed, and Rhain's heart clenched for her pain, and his own.

An hour later, they were smoothly slipping into a dock surrounded by the sooty miasma belched from a sugarcane rendering factory.

The port appeared lawless. Whores flashed skin, white, brown, and black. Breasts on display. A handful of sailors on the ship docked next to theirs sent taunting jeers, vulgar gestures, and bare arses wiggling at them.

Lydia tsked and turned from the view. "This place is vile. Resembles a madhouse. It is lawless. Are you certain we are in the right place?"

He kissed her knuckles. "You can be assured that I will make certain of that before you have to dirty your pretty dress." His flippant tone was meant to amuse her, but next he said seriously, "Stay on board, Lyd. Until I ascertain the situation. Yes?"

"Yes," she agreed.

He wound his way through the crowds, past bedraggled men and women, many struggling with handcarts, some with wheels that wobbled precariously; other carts were pulled and limped sideways, like they were about to topple, pivoting on a center axle that chewed small chunks out of the planking of the dock.

Poverty permeated the very air here, with the grim and desperate looks on the workers' faces. It was apparent they lived from one moment to the next. No work, no pay, no food.

One man strutted across the wharf with a mission. Long gray hair under his cap bounced in the breeze. His jaunty step suggested a recent windfall. Or perhaps he was on his way to meet a lover.

A lover.

All of a sudden his lungs clenched tight. It was impossible to take a deep breath. The realization that he would likely never see Alastair after today nearly sent him to his knees. Leaning against a pylon, he tried to regain his bearings. One breath. Two. Three.

Pushing away from the supporting post, he stood on his own feet, took a breath, then continued on his quest. It did not matter what his body desired; what mattered was making a home for Lydia and himself.

Once determined, it took no time at all to find the local acting port authority among the querulous crowd; he simply looked for the cleanest face in the throng, which turned out to be a young man by the name of Thomas Green. A soft-spoken and highly competent man, he assured Rhain that the situation on the island was calm, except at the port town. Apparently, the storm brought all the people with damaged homes and injuries here for help. The excitement of the storm and the crowding turned some people rough and loud, the man said. Once outside town, everything is orderly and reconstruction is underway.

He hated to ask, but he needed to know. "Was anyone killed?"

"I'm afraid so. We don't know how many yet, but my guess is several hundred."

"Thank you for your help, sir," he said as he fought the tightness in his neck and shoulders. He hoped his plantation and foreman were undamaged and unhurt. He wished he were a good enough person to say his concern stemmed from compassion to the people harmed, but he knew deep down that he was not such a good person. His main concern was for Lydia's continued comfort.

Forcing his worry away, Rhain admitted the man impressed him with his helpfulness, even sending a wagon and driver to convey them and their belongings to the plantation. Rhain set aside his concerns and directed the unloading and reloading of their belongings onto the large, two-horse wagon. The thing did not seem all that sturdy, but it did hold up under the weight of their crates.

That done, there was nothing left to do but gather up Lydia and wish a farewell to the crew. At the thought, Rhain's optimism died a bright, vivid death.

* * * *

Alastair stood by and watched the whole exchange. Rhain, that young fool, was really going to leave and take his fragile sister with him. The damn, damn fool.

He met Rhain as the man came up the gangplank. "A moment of your time?"

"Certainly, Captain. In fact, I came to see you and to collect Lydia." He smiled and looked much too young to be going off alone with no one to protect him and his sister.

He came to say good-bye? A brief painful lurch occupied his chest, and he could not speak momentarily. He took that time to steer Rhain to a more private location so they could talk quietly.

Behind a few well-placed barrels, he pulled Rhain close and caressed the silky surface of his clean muslin shirt. "The environment here is not right. I have rarely seen a town so out of control."

"Not to worry, the mayhem is only due to the storm damage and the plantation workers swarming the city for help. The port authority told me all about it; he is quite accommodating in fact, and said things will settle in a few days."

"Rhain—"

"Don't worry, Alastair. I will whisk Lydia out of town right away, and we will be safely at our plantation and away from the rabble in no time. I was assured all is safe."

"Be that as it may, I think it will be safer for Lydia to stay here, with your belongings. I can send an armed escort with you until you make certain all is well at your estate."

The infuriating boy laughed. "Says the man who scoffs at storms and chases other ships. I thought you were fearless."

He allowed that compliment to fill his aching heart, but he would not be distracted. "I must admit I am worried about the two of you."

"You think I can't take care of myself and Lydia? That we need a governess? We don't need your services any longer, Captain. But if truth were told, I worry at times that I'm not capable enough. Right now, I want to fall into your arms and let you take care of everything. But I cannot do that. I belong on land, Lydia belongs on land, and I must get this plantation working for both our sakes."

"Damn you, boy. You are not thinking clearly; your head is in the clouds about your *land*, so you can't see the danger around you." Not the best thing to say, especially after Rhain had just opened up and expressed a weakness. Exposed his underbelly, so to speak.

Rhain's temper and pride obviously got the better of him. He puffed his chest out and scowled.

No one would be able to convince him at this point. Alastair knew him well enough to surmise that much.

So all he said was, "We will be here for seven days if you have need of anything." Or if you just want to see me, he thought. "The crew needs some shore leave." He lied. The only reason they would stay in this hellhole was to make available a safe retreat for the two underprepared landowners.

In the end, they parted in anger. The last thing he hoped to accomplish. But perhaps in the long run anger would make it easier for both of them.

* * * *

Rhain hurt.

Every single piece of him hurt, from the inside out. Including his hair. Even so, he held his head high as he helped Lydia leave the ship. Why had he held on to his pride and left Alastair furious instead of kissing the man stupid?

"Ouch," Lydia said and tried to yank her arm out of his viselike grip.

He let go immediately. "I am very sorry, dear. Wasn't paying attention."

She glared at him for what must have been the twentieth time that day.

God, he felt awful. He didn't realize leaving Alastair, knowing he would likely never see the man again, would be so difficult. He wanted to turn around and head back up the gangplank to the man, grab him, and take him directly to bed. He ran a shaking hand over his sweat-slicked face.

The man said he loved him. Of course, the words were uttered during a heated fuck and meant nothing. Alastair had been carried away by the intensity of the moment, that was all. However, at the time…it meant the world to Rhain. He wanted, needed, more time. Time to enjoy, time to see where this could lead. Time they didn't have. So there was no chance to determine how deeply he loved. After all, he thought he'd loved Robert once.

They reached the wagon where two of Alastair's sailors stood about, making certain nothing was stolen. He handed Lydia up on the wagon seat. She slid to the middle next to the driver and fluffed her skirts, still not looking at him.

Knowing it was a monumentally bad idea but unable to stop himself, he looked back at the ship, at Alastair. The man looked as stoic and beautiful as he had the first night they'd met. Now, standing at the quarterdeck, one foot propped on the lowest rail, a hand holding an overhead rope, he could have been the King of England himself, for all the power he held over Rhain at that moment.

He couldn't breathe. Blinking rapidly, he rubbed at his constricted throat.

Alastair leaned forward a few inches, his hand flexing on the rope.

Call me back. Call us both back.

There was no last-minute declaration of love or even longing. Which was for the best. Rhain turned, climbed into the wagon, and told the driver to, well, drive.

There was a bounce of the boards. He looked back. One leathery sailor had hopped on the back. Looking up in time, he saw Alastair point to another, toothless, sailor, who immediately jumped on the overloaded wagon as well.

Rhain glared at the seamen as one of them started singing an off-key ditty about an amply chested woman.

They rolled away, leaving the *Hurricane* behind.

* * * *

Alastair clasped and unclasped the rough rope and watched the stretch of road where Rhain and his ragtag group disappeared not five minutes before, telling himself no one would follow them to murder, rape, and steal all their belongings.

"I can't believe that young fool," Dunn snarled in Alastair's ear. "The damn foul air is already starting up Lydia's cough."

Alastair whipped his head around at the slur on his lover's name, but Dunn continued.

"And I don't like the feel of things. Too much riffraff peddling and sneaking about. Tells me there is no or very corrupt law and too much poverty."

He agreed.

"Poverty leads to violence. Why did you let them go?"

"What choice did I have? What? You want me to cuff Rhain—Mr. Morgan—in irons and leave him shackled with Balls?" His response was much too heated, he could tell from Dunn's startled expression, but damn, he had never felt so helpless.

"We are staying for seven days. Arrange the crew's watches."

Dunn spluttered.

"I want to be here if those two need help."

"Captain, this place is a powder keg. You certain we can safely stay for seven days?"

"I don't know, but I'm not leaving those two young lambs in this wolf's den until I know they have a safe place to retreat if needed."

"Good idea, sir." Dunn squeezed his shoulder in a rare show of support.

Chapter Twelve

They never drove out of the pall of smoke. The miasma from the cane rendering plant sank into the rutted path.

No one with a sane mind could call what they traveled on a road. It looked more like a wet, sloppy clearing between the ever-present tall, mud-coated grasses that obscured any view.

The place stank like London and looked like a madman's crazed idea of a maze.

Every few miles they passed a slapdash hut made of cane stalks lashed together with fronds or thin rope. Always the hut sat in a small muddy clearing.

There were many swollen rivers and streams with wildly wobbly bridges to traverse. One so unstable, Lydia cried out in fear.

"Not to worry, miss," the driver said. "A crew worked all yesterday shorin' everthin' up. Won't be no bridge that can't take our little load."

The words were hardly believable, but they did make it over unscathed.

Nothing taller than about ten feet was left standing; everything else had succumbed to the hurricane winds.

Large areas were covered with mudslide debris, making the landscape appear similar to what he imagined the bottom of a lake would look like.

Occasionally heaps of a mud flow had been dug out to allow carts to pass on the trail.

"Why was so much labor taken to clear this path just after the storm? I would think all efforts would be on helping the injured and shoring up homes."

"Aye, people are doin' that as well. But landowners want to send their downed cane to the plant while it still holds sap. Otherwise they won't have a crop this season. I'll pick up a load to take down with me on the return trip. This isn't cane-cutting season, so it won't have much sap in it this time o'year. They will receive little for their efforts, but some is better than nothin', I suppose."

"Did our crop sustain damage, do you know?"

The driver hacked and then spat a large wad over the side of the wagon. "Don't believe you oughter worry about that, Mr. Morgan."

No? Well then, that was good news. Their little slice of land must be in a prime location to have survived the mudslides and wind damage. He smiled to himself and looked forward to getting out of the jarring wagon and off the boulder-hard seat.

The longer they traveled, hitting potholes every few yards, the smaller Lydia appeared. She'd started coughing before they left the ship, and the cough grew louder with each passing mile.

Goddamn. He hoped they would rise out of this miasma before she became feverish.

He wrapped an arm around her thin shoulders. "Just around the corner, I'm certain there will be a nice hill that takes us to our plantation. It will be green and lush and will capture the ocean breeze. You'll see. It will be a paradise, just like we talked about."

They passed no other wagons, no other horses with riders, and the only sound other than their ragged crew, were insects chirping and whirring, the sound unlike anything he'd ever heard before.

Lydia snuggled against his chest and shuddered with a sob.

Some twenty minutes later, they were not in paradise; in fact, he suspected they couldn't be much closer to hell.

* * * *

Alastair and Dunn were in their third cobbled-together punch house in as many hours. In each, they gleaned information to piece together the current affairs. In each, a handful of men asked, some begged, to be taken on as hands in exchange for transporting their wives and children.

He would never hire any of the rum sots, but he did feel sorry for their families.

The increasingly angry comments to their questions stirred up vitriol against the governor. In essence, the people were close to riot, if not outright war.

Alastair's worries were nothing compared to the reality of this poor island.

The government was corrupt and did not even hide its attempts at stealing everyone's money. Landowners were pulling out and slaves fleeing. The island was enveloped in turmoil. The locals feared a revolt, but the government, all fat and bloated, acted invincible. They probably thought they were, with their rifles and colorful uniforms.

"What should we do? Go and retrieve the Morgans?"

"No," Alastair told Dunn. "We can't force them to leave this hellhole. And I suspect they don't have the money with which to settle someplace else." He drummed his finger on a tankard of ale he had not the stomach for.

Dunn rocked his head back and forth in his hands. "There will be a civil war here before the month is up," he whispered.

"The Morgans are not safe here, I agree." He tapped a finger on the sticky table. What could they do to convince Rhain to extract his sister and his handsome arse off this island with their skin still attached? "If you asked Miss Lydia to leave with us without Rhain's permission, would she?"

Dunn shook his head again. "I don't think so. She adores her brother. Thinks he hangs the stars every night. Damn the luck I'd fall in love with a girl who won't leave her brother's side for anything. Guess he earned her devotion by taking care of her through that damn illness."

Alastair nodded even though Dunn couldn't see. "You love her, then? I thought as much."

"Who in their bleedin' right mind wouldn't love her? Well, anyone who sought women that is. Beg pardon."

"No offense taken."

Dunn slugged back the rest of his dark and tart rum punch. "She is so accepting. Never passes judgment. She even kissed Tim without thinking anything could be considered wrong with it." He laughed. "She is simply wonderful. Would have preferred she'd not kissed Tim, though. Should have come straight to me."

"I think more than half the ship would protect her with their last breath, Dunn." He smiled, realizing he was in the majority. He also realized she accepted the unusual because of her brother's gentle and loving care. A brother who on the surface displayed spines and thorns, but Alastair knew those prickles stemmed from protecting Miss Lydia. On his own, he would be a much sweeter, more accepting man.

He missed the boy already, and it had barely been half a day since he watched that damn wagon wobble off with its one warped wheel.

"So how are we going to entice them both back on ship before this bloody island explodes into civil war?"

"Kidnap them both tonight," Dunn said.

"Too late and too dark to find them."

"Then we kidnap them in the morning."

"Kidnapping *is* against the law, you know, my dear cutthroat. And even more importantly, they would both hate us after that. Not the outcome I would like."

"No, I suppose not."

"Any other helpful ideas?" Alastair was fresh out of them at the moment, so he really hoped Dunn could come up with something.

"Here we go! How 'bout we stage a revolt and show up at their plantation just at the right time to save them. Then they both love us forever after we whisk them back to the ship. We leave after our fake revolutionaries wash up, change clothes, and return to ship."

Suppressing a smile, Alastair stoically said, "Very good idea. But I do imagine the Morgans would at some point hear of our duplicity. Maybe we can think of something more direct and honest. For I fear anything else would not be acceptable to those two."

"Yep. Too many scruples between them."

Alastair agreed.

"Well, then, we could simply proclaim our love and whisk them away to a life at sea."

A grand idea. All of a sudden Alastair lost his desire to move. He could wallow here on the damn filthy table and drink his life away, because he *had* declared his love. And he'd been rejected

Dunn proved to be more imaginative than he himself. The best he could come up with was to let Rhain see for himself how bad things were and then come begging for a place on ship.

What a fool he was to think that proud boy would ever do such a thing.

Pulling himself together, he said, "Let's go back to the ship. I don't think that is a workable plan, either. Tomorrow we will figure something out." Because something must work, he thought.

He clapped his hand on Dunn's shoulder, and they left for the ship.

* * * *

The plantation was a disaster.

A disaster.

All his hopes, his dreams. To make a good life for Lydia. To be a respected landowner.

Rhain stared at the small clearing, swallowing hard. He was afraid he'd disgrace himself in front of everyone and lose his meager supper of hard cheese and even harder bread. But who would really care if he cast up his accounts? Lydia had seen him vomit before, the seamen would be gone tomorrow, and the retainers...the retainers. They were another matter entirely.

The two small, wiry men sat in the shade, sharing a pipe. Their ancestral origins were hard to identify with the layer of dirt on their sun-darkened skin. A shack was the only building in sight, with no door aside from a tattered blanket tacked up over the opening, and no windows.

One of the drug-addled men claimed to be the foreman, but Rhain couldn't imagine this man corresponding with him.

He'd asked why there were no crops planted and where they could find the main house.

The foreman informed him there was no money left. No help. So they didn't plant crops. He pointed to the shack. "This is the main house."

"What happened to the previous two or three year's revenue?" Rhain struggled to keep his voice just below a bellow.

The foreman shrugged. "Most of it were took by the new gov'ners taxes. We got enough left to eat on for the next few months; then it all be gone." The man's singsong speech could be due to the drug, or to English not being his native tongue.

"Why is this the first I've heard of the situation?"

"I don't read and write, so I answered your letters through the gov'ner's office. Perhaps they are not very good at writing neither."

"Your letter said there was a large, sturdy house."

"Yes." The man gave a long sigh. "This were a grand improvement. After it were built, the workers and I had a place out of the rain and away from the biters." At that, the foreman slapped a blood-juicy mosquito on his forearm. "Keep us dry through this last storm, it did."

"Your letters said we would have good crops this year and you would implement more improvements."

"Yes, things would have been good this year, and we planned to fix the well."

"Except?"

"Except the taxes."

Rhain was five very short seconds from strangling the man who stood in front of him, his dark face content and relaxed, likely from whatever it was they smoked. And how the bloody hell had he been able to afford or to cultivate a drug and not sugarcane?

The worthless foreman said, "Would you like me to show you the improvements?"

He gritted his teeth. "Yes."

The man did show him, with what seemed to be great pride. He showed that the house had four walls, a cloth door to keep the insects out, and the most amazing part—a wooden roof. He smiled when he said it could house sixteen workers and keep them out of the rain while they slept.

Rhain wondered what those sixteen workers ever accomplished.

* * * *

Lydia still sat in the wagon, looking like a drowned kitten, her yellow muslin dress and pale curls plastered to her skin from the heat and humidity.

The place lacked the beauty they'd seen on other islands. Their small plot of land was a flat spot between large hills. The sun baked the area, making the clearing feel like a soup bowl over flame. It was hot and muggy.

It was miserable.

There was no cooling breeze tickling his ear, and there were tall, ugly grasses that blocked any view. No trees or inviting green meadows, only a few slimy ponds, and insects. God, he had never seen so many insects. They swarmed him every time he stopped moving. And the least charming of it all—the pall of nasty, putrid smoke from the refinery hovered just over their heads.

He walked, stiff-legged, to the wagon.

One seaman asked, "Where should we put the crates and luggage?" The other leathery man curled his upper lip and looked around at their little slice of hell.

The driver just seemed bored.

"Are you certain this is *our* plantation?" Lydia said, her words squeaked out of constricted lungs.

The foreman said, "Aye, miss, this is owned by a Mr. Morgan."

At the confirmation, Lydia sank further into herself and coughed into a soiled handkerchief.

"It will be dark soon. Will there be a moon tonight?"

The driver shook his head. "Afraid not, sir. Too dark. Can't go back to port until morning. Otherwise I might drive off into a flooded riverbank."

He sighed. His shoulders felt like they weighed two hundred pounds each. "Well, let's make the most of it and make this shack presentable for Miss Lydia. Take these crates into the...*house*."

He watched as the men carried all their worldly possessions into the shack. Ten crates, their clothing, and this worthless bit of land. That was all they had left.

"Well, on the bright side, our new home isn't covered by a mudslide."

Lydia did not laugh.

"Don't worry, dear, we will go back to Roseau first thing in the morning and talk to the officials. We will figure out what is going on here." Fortunately, he was able to sound much more convinced than he felt.

Chapter Thirteen

Rhain pried his eyes open and blinked away sleep. The dark outline of a windowless room slowly took form. *The shack. Damn.*

He'd slept quite soundly, which was a surprise since he spent the night with only a few blankets on a hard-packed earthen floor. Of course, it was the first time he'd slept on land in more than two months. Perhaps the stillness rocked him to sleep, so to speak. That, or not being tempted to wake and make love to Alastair several times throughout the night.

Standing, he stretched and yawned; his jaw popped. He adjusted his clothing and glanced over to check on Lydia.

She was wrapped in a tumble of blankets on the pathetic pallet they'd made yesterday evening. The only thing visible on the girl was her nose, closed eyes, and a tuft of mussed hair. She snored softly, the sound holding an alarming amount of congestion.

Leaving her to sleep, he went to the bucket of almost clean water, drank, and then washed himself as best he could. He needed to be presentable when he talked with the government officials today to straighten out the problem with their estate and the damn taxes.

Stepping around one of their crates, he went outside to the already oppressively hot day. He organized the men and made notes on what they needed to purchase while in town.

Half an hour later, Lydia stepped into the sun-scalded day, wrapped in a blanket, her hair still sleep-rumpled. Shivering and coughing, she climbed into the wagon.

He climbed in after her and squeezed her hand. "We'll find a nice place for you to stay until this damn smoke clears." He waved his hand, indicating the air around them that was thick with soot. "I'm certain this is a seasonal occurrence and we will breathe good, clean air once the wind changes and blows the smoke out to sea. Or even better, when they are done rendering the cane." He ignored the driver's snort.

Yesterday the foreman confirmed his worst fear that when the crops were good, the cane plant ran nine months out of the year. Perhaps this hadn't been a good year for cane crops. The other bad news had been finding out the prevailing wind direction was the one they were currently experiencing. There was no use telling this to Lydia at the moment, when she felt so terrible and grieved the loss of Dunn.

"Until the air clears, you will be staying on the outskirts of town, in a nice, clean boarding house for women, with fresh air and nice young ladies to talk with. Would you like that?"

Lydia only nodded and rested her head on his shoulder.

An establishment nice enough for Lydia to stay in would be dreadfully expensive. He must find the funds to keep her safe and make the plantation productive as well. He would ask about a loan, and he would ask the governor himself, if needed, to recheck their tax burden and offer a reimbursement for what he was convinced must be a mistake. If all else failed, he could sell his pianoforte. But not Lydia's harp. He could never do that to her.

He brushed a lock of sweaty hair off her heated forehead. "It will all be fine, dear. Have faith."

This time she didn't even nod.

* * * *

Rhain waited for a quarter hour in a windowless, dark-paneled room which reminded him of a tomb, before being ushered in to see Lieutenant Governor Wilkins. He suspected the short wait had more to do with how many taxes he had paid the past two years than it did with his social standing as landowner.

Wilkins was a short, round man with jowls like a mastiff, which jiggled as he hurried around a large mahogany desk. "Mr. Morgan, what a pleasure to make your acquaintance. I must say it was a surprise to learn you would move to your plantation. A pleasant surprise for certain." He grabbed Rhain's outstretched hand and gave him a firm but damp handshake.

"A pleasure to meet you as well, Lieutenant Governor."

"I hope the storm did no damage to your property," the man said in practiced sincerity.

"Very little it seems. We are in a protected spot between two large hills, but I must say I was distressed that only grasses and scrub grow on my land."

"Oh. Terrible, terrible."

"Indeed. Seems I have a small problem about my tax rate that I'm certain was a mistake, and I'd like to see this matter resolved as quickly as possible, as I need the funds for improvements and men to work my fields. I'm sure you understand that without a crop, I will not be able to pay further taxes."

"Quite right, quite right. Must harvest the crop before having taxable revenue; we in the government understand that with certainty."

The man seemed quite interested in helping, so it was frustrating to spend the better part of an hour on social niceties, gossip, and a discussion about their local horse-racing track, which the official assured him would be up and running in a week. Two at most.

"Very interesting, thank you for sharing information about Dominica, sir. I wonder if we can work on my tax issue. I'd like to go around to the shops before they close to purchase a few necessary items."

"Of course, of course." The man hefted himself out of his chair with the help of both hands on the armrests, then went to a large bookshelf and extracted three leather-bound tomes. "Let's see here, these should have the information we need." He dumped the books on the substantial desk and started flipping through the pages. Several "Oh, I sees" and many "hmms" later, the man closed the last book and looked directly at Rhain.

"I think I can see a place or two where your tax rate may have been a tad miscalculated. I will write a short report for the governor for his consideration and will let you know the decision as soon as I hear more."

"What excellent news." Rhain knew things would start to go their way. It just took perseverance and good manners. Feeling better than he had since they floated into this harbor, he left the office and went to find someone to dig a deep well for his property.

He was standing outside the last of three shops, gritting his teeth, when he heard the loveliest sound this cursed island could generate.

"There you are, Mr. Morgan," Alastair shouted from down the street.

They hurried to meet each other, shook hands, and slapped backs as if they were long-lost brothers seeing each other after years of separation. Rhain smiled so wide his sunburned lower lip split open, but he didn't care. Still shaking Alastair's hand, his tongue took over before his brain even knew he was going to speak. "Damn, but I missed you last night."

Alastair sported an unsteady smile. "Did you? I had thought... Never mind. I am very glad you missed me. I missed you as well." His next words were smooth as silk and promised passion. "Come to the ship. I have something to discuss with you."

Although he hadn't time to spend in his captain's arms, that was exactly what Rhain desired more than anything. But he still needed to purchase provisions and return to the plantation before dark. It was already close to four. He could not linger in Roseau, even for such a sweet offer as another evening with his beloved Alastair.

"With regret, I must decline. I still have things to buy before the shops close. Can you believe the price of everything on this muddy, godforsaken rock?"

"I know. Everything about this damn island is wrong. Rhain, I've been looking for you for over an hour; we really must talk. Come to the ship with me?"

Rhain's heart stuttered at the thought of just what passion they would unleash if he went back to the ship. He struggled with temptation.

"I wish I could, but..." He shook his head.

Alastair stopped and looked at him. His expression closed off, so Rhain couldn't begin to determine what the man thought. "What if I give you enough provisions for a week and have one of my men find you a ride? Then will you come?"

He smiled at that. Alastair really was very persuasive. "Well, that does solve the problem nicely. Thank you, I will come with you. But I can only stay for a short while so I can say good night to Lydia before it is too dark to maneuverer a wagon to my plantation. Lydia is staying with a family named Hancock. They are a respectable household with three daughters and room to spare. We were fortunate to find them by word of mouth. She will stay there until things are settled." The comment was only partially true, and he felt guilty about lying.

With his lips pressed into a flat line and eyes half closed, Alastair looked like he would say something Rhain did not want to hear. Instead the man said, "Come then, I will explain when we are there."

They hurried through town, shoved their way through the raucous crowd on the dock, and were on the ship within a quarter of the clock. A sudden release of tension and a feeling of contentment washed over him as soon as he stepped off the gangplank. It felt like coming home after a year abroad. How strange, that.

The air was clear here. At least for the moment. The ocean breeze blew the damn soot onto his property but left the air around the dock sea-salt fresh. He was enjoying a deep lungful when Lydia appeared from the belowdeck hatch and walked over to him. She kept one hand on the rail and one hand on her chest, breathing shallowly; still, she looked healthier than she had since setting foot on Dominica.

"Oh, good, the captain found you." Her voice sounded quiet and raspy. "I worried he would miss you and you'd learn of my decision from the letter I left in my room."

Now if that statement didn't leave his heart lurching from fear, then nothing ever would. "Lydia?"

She grabbed both of his hands and squeezed harder than he thought she could. "Rhain, this island is not safe. The captain and Conall talked to just about everyone in Roseau, and it is common knowledge there have been many slave uprisings in the past six months."

"That may be, dear. However, the port authority and the lieutenant governor assured me everything has been resolved and this disturbance will be over soon. I think it is simply a result of the storm."

"Yes, well, that must be what the governor is telling them to say so they can keep everyone on the island. Conall told me that people, especially estate owners and business men, are leaving as fast as they can book passage. In fact, something close to thirty people have asked for passage on the *Hurricane*. It is madness down there." She waved her hand at the teeming wharf, where just then a man with his arm around a young woman holding a baby yelled up at them, asking if they had room for additional passengers. "You see," she exclaimed breathily. She coughed then, but sounded better than when he'd left her that morning.

"Lydia, no matter where you live, there is always someone grumbling about possible uprisings. It is the way people are. They always—"

"Be silent and listen to me."

His sister was a sweet girl; she never talked to anyone that way, especially not to him. "My…dear?"

"This place is headed toward civil war before end of the year, mark my words. The dispossessed are going to take what they feel belongs to them, and the government is too weak to do anything about it. In fact, the captain learned that the official port ship is prepared to leave at a moment's notice. The government is afraid; the people are afraid. You noticed it. So let us leave. We can stay on the *Hurricane* until things settle here; then you can come back."

His blood froze in his veins despite the unbearable temperature. "What. Do. You. Mean. *I* can come back?"

Just then Dunn stepped up beside Lydia and put his hand on her shoulder. "I've asked your sister for her hand in marriage."

Alastair held him back before his forward momentum launched him at the goddamn first mate. "No. You bloody damn will not marry my sister."

He almost slipped from Alastair's grasp and lunged again, and they both ended up on the oak planking. He refused to punch Alastair, and that was likely the only way he would pull free. Realizing they would progress nowhere if he didn't stop trying to kill scum water First Mate Conall Dunn, he snarled, "Let me up. I am almost certain I will not try to kill him. Not yet anyway."

Alastair didn't look convinced, but he did let Rhain up.

"Take a walk with me, Lyd."

They left the two men, but he could feel their eyes burning into his back as they toured the perimeter of the ship, with Tim following them not two steps behind the whole time.

"I have accepted Conall's offer. I find I quite love the man. I like sailing, and I feel good on the ship. Feel better than I have since my illness started. If I tire of sailing, then he has a home in the country, and he assures me the air there is as sweet as I am." She giggled and blushed, despite the dreadful situation.

"Rhain, can you not support my decision and be happy for me?"

"No, Lydia. You are a gently bred woman; he was born in the stews. For the love of God, don't you see how many ways this is ridiculous?"

She stopped and turned to him. Tim stood behind her, hand on the hilt of a wicked-looking dagger. Lydia's expression was pinched and stubborn as she said, "His mother was not a whore; she washed clothes to feed her children. He is a good man and deserves respect. You have seen that."

He couldn't argue her point. "That is not enough for a successful marriage. What will you do if you swell with pregnancy? He will leave you in a port, and you'll see him every other year for a week or two. You will be poor, probably with a dozen children that he will forget the names of. Who will take care of you when you're sick, Lyd? No, I cannot accept this. It is wrong for you, and I will not allow it."

Her words were wrapped in steel when she told him, "I hoped to have your approval, but I will do this with or without it. We are not in England anymore.

"Now go and collect our crates; we will sail this evening, as it is unsafe for you to be here. If you do not want to stay on ship, Alastair said he knows of a few towns that will be more to your liking until this island settles down and is safe again."

"Lydia, I am not leaving, and I will not let you leave either. You must realize this is madness, and as your brother I cannot let this happen."

"Good-bye, brother. Stay safe." She turned on her heel and stomped off to go belowdeck.

"Lydia, pack your things; I am taking you off this damnable boat."

Her white-topped head disappeared, and he had a feeling he would have to drag her off with an armed escort.

Alastair took that moment to walk over and talk to him, but he was not in an accommodating mood.

"Rhain, I would love nothing more than to have you stay with me on this ship, in whatever capacity you'd like." He cupped Rhain's cheek. "I have fallen in love with you, and I ask that you go with us." He swallowed hard, but Rhain refused to look at him. "I can't leave you here. I can't bear the thought of you getting hurt, or worse. Stay with me. For a little while at least. Until this unrest is over."

He looked at Alastair, then. The man was so beautiful, it hurt to see him. And for a few foolish heartbeats, he allowed himself to dream.

Leaving him for the second time was the hardest thing he would ever do. "I'm going to help Lydia pack, and then I am taking her back to her rented room where she belongs, and I am going to my plantation where I belong."

"She wants to stay. I will not let you force her to leave." He gripped Rhain's arm lightly.

Rhain brushed it off and headed for the belowdeck hatch. Before he knew what was going on, eight sailors stood between him and his goal. He tried to step past them, but they refused to budge.

He spun around and glared at Alastair.

Dunn now stood beside the captain, face set and unyielding.

"I will bring the army and take her off this damn ship if you don't let me take her now."

His voice dead and flat, Alastair said, "We will be gone as soon as your feet hit the wharf."

And he knew that would be true. There was nothing he could do.

Rhain left the ship, jumped onto the provision-laden horse cart Alastair arranged, and then rode off the wharf, never looking back at the sister and pirate who held his heart.

Chapter Fourteen

One month later. November.

Rhain sat on one of his unpacked crates, head in hands, and experienced the fear he'd fought for so long creep over him. The dark tendrils drilled into his brain and soul, waking nightmares he'd suppressed for years.

Yelling for control, he stood, trembling.

The island was at war, the slaves in revolt. Many people were dead; many more had left the island. He'd traveled to the capital to see if he could help care for the injured that continued to flood into the city from the countryside, but there was chaos and fighting and no medical supplies, so nothing was achieved. Finally, he'd gone back to his plantation, where he housed some children who seemed abandoned. And then one night, the foreman and the children simply disappeared, leaving him completely alone.

There was no one to plant, which was good really because there would be no one to harvest either. The island was in anarchy, and he had absolutely no idea what to do.

Roseau was governed by gangs, and no ships were allowed to dock since the Navy stationed a warship at the mouth of the harbor, warning other ships away. The only good thing that came from all this was the damn cane refinery stopped pumping smoke into the air.

But these were all trivial matters. His worst fear was coming true as he slowly rotted in this godforsaken hut; he would never be able to tell Alastair that he was worthy of love. That someone, he, loved Alastair with all his being.

He scratched at his sunburned and insect-bitten forearm. If he hadn't been so arrogant and had listened to Lydia, he could be having supper with the irresistible man right now, getting ready for a night of lovemaking.

Sighing, he stood and took count of his remaining food stock. He would have enough for one more week if he started half rations tomorrow.

Then what would he do? Eat grass. He snorted. There was certainly plenty of that commodity around.

He had nothing of real value, had no one, no future, and he feared he slowly slipped into madness.

Lydia, he hoped, would do well and was happy. God, what he wouldn't do to see her smiling face again, and to see Alastair.

"What a stupid arse I am." How could he have left the man he was so thoroughly in love with? Why hadn't he returned the wonderful words to his pirate before leaving the ship?

If he lived through this damn civil war, he would find them, and if either of them would have him after he'd acted like a tyrant, then he would never let them go again.

Of course, Alastair probably hated him now, since he'd refused the gift so freely given. He walked out of the hut, hoping to catch a cool breeze as he continued to castigate himself. "I am such a stupid arse," he said out loud just to hear something other than the ever-present insects.

"I don't know. You do have some intelligent moments."

Rhain stumbled to a halt and watched Alastair stroll up to his shack, about ten sailors with hand carts and another twenty with wicked-looking weapons following behind.

"Alastair!" He launched himself toward the swaggering man and nearly toppled him. The pirate laughed until Rhain silenced him with a healthy, smacking kiss. He laughed and then went in for another, this one long and slow.

"Well, now that is almost worth the damn trip through this hellhole swamp. However, I'll expect more later." He held Rhain's shoulders and pushed him at arm's length. "Have you had enough of this place yet? Ready to come away with me?"

Rhain smiled.

"That looks like a yes; please tell me that is a yes. If I return to the ship without you, I'm afraid Mrs. Dunn will toss me overboard."

"So they are married now."

Alastair nodded and watched him as if expecting a blow.

He sighed, figuring that was an inevitable outcome and probably not as tragic a consequence as he'd once thought. "Is she well…and content?"

"Come see for yourself, but I think you will be happy with what you see."

He decided not to make a decision just yet. His brain felt stuffed with cotton. "How are you here? The Roseau harbor is closed."

"Never fear; when pirates want something, they find a way to take it. I'll tell you as my men load up your stuff, hmm?"

In the end, it was easier to let Alastair make the decision for him. They went into the shack, and he showed them what to take and what to leave as Alastair told him that they anchored close to shore about two miles away.

"Cutting through the ever-present damn grass was the hardest part, until we reached the road we could see through our spyglasses. The two old seamen I sent to the plantation with you have very good senses of direction and led us here with ease."

With everything loaded, Rhain took one long last look at his land, not certain he would ever see it again. Not even certain if he ever wished to see it again. Then he turned his back and started down the dusty trail, Alastair walking right alongside him.

"You should not have come for me. You are already so far behind in your route and losing money because of your delays."

Alastair looked at him sideways. "Such is the way with shipping. What we lose one year we make up another. Besides, I ferried some cargo back and forth between islands that I had not expected to gain. It will help us. Lydia believes we will break even this year. She is turning out to be a fine purser and indeed found some funds I did not realize I still had."

"She is a marvel, is she not?" He smiled. He would see Lydia again soon. Alastair and Lydia, all in one day. His heart flipped.

"Rhain," Alastair said, and his next words slipped out slow and hesitant, "I find myself in need of a sturdy yardman. Thought you might know of someone in need of work."

"That depends; what does the position pay?"

"Nightly buggering."

That shook a sharp, quick laugh out of him, and he realized he hadn't laughed since the day Alastair left Roseau without him. "Well, then, we might be able to work something out. Although that will mean I have to become used to that infernal constant noise again."

He stopped and let the seamen with hand carts catch up to them. When the largest crate rolled by on a sturdy cart pushed by two of the burliest men, he patted the side. He had lugged that crate halfway around the world but hadn't seen its contents for months. "Is it possible to fit a pianoforte in the galley, do you think?"

His pirate smiled, showing about one hundred, beautiful, white teeth. "For you, love, anything."

Chapter Fifteen

The pianoforte did in fact fit in the galley, as did Lydia's harp. They were both somewhat battered now, as they'd bolted them to the floor to keep them from moving during rough seas, but Rhain didn't care. Tonight, one week after leaving Dominica, they played for more than an hour, entertaining as much of the crew as could squeeze into the galley and hallway.

It felt good to play again, and even though the pianoforte was horribly out of tune, the crew didn't seem to mind in the slightest, and it was something he and Lydia—Mrs. Dunn, he reminded himself—could fix with a few tools purchased in any large town.

It was still strange thinking of Lydia as married, but she seemed content with Dunn, and acting as purser gave her a sense of accomplishment. Her cheeks stayed pink, and she laughed often. He could not be happier for her, and he'd made amends with Dunn, mostly. He still couldn't move past the notion that the man screwed his little sister. That, he was sure, would bother him until they were both wrinkled and gray. For the first time in years, he actually anticipated Lydia living to see old age. Her strength and health had returned with nary a cough or fever.

The galley was now empty save for him. He polished the pianoforte and enjoyed a few rare moments of solitude.

"The crew inform me that you are a terrible yardman, and they suggest you should be the entertainment officer." Alastair lounged against the door frame, looking so much like the first day Rhain met him. Tall, bold, and beautiful. White shirt billowy and laces loose around his neck. That vibrant leather belt just begging to be removed.

He laughed. "That sounds like a pastime, not a career. I've continued studying navigation."

"Have you?"

"Yes, actually. I devoured your book while still on ship and purchased a few that second day in that godforsaken port town."

"That is splendid, as it is my least favorite part of sailing."

They smiled at each other then. Certainly they would look stupid to any observer, but he couldn't bring himself to care—he was content for the first time in his adult life.

"With everything that has gone on, I forgot to ask what you ever did with Balls."

Alastair looked down at his boots. When he did finally speak, his voice was quiet, without inflection, as if this were a chore he dreaded but knew was coming. "That overly large waste of skin finally admitted he planned to take over the ship. He said as bold as you please that if he had killed you, Dunn, and me, he could have convinced the crew to go along with him as captain." He snorted. "Ludicrous. That man didn't have the brains to guide a skiff, much less a ship. After that we could not shut the man up. He was a terror, trying to instigate a mutiny by talking to anyone who would happen by. Even got a few of the new hands to halfheartedly agree to help him. I tossed him and his accomplice off the ship when we left Tortola."

"You what?"

"Now don't fret about Balls. We were close to shore, and he was—is—an excellent swimmer. I am certain the other lad probably was also. By now Balls has probably swived his way through at least half the population of sodomites on that damn island and is figuring out if he has the stamina to swive the rest of the men by week's end. Don't feel sorry for him. He made his fate and has most likely joined the Brethren of the Coast already."

He didn't feel sorry for the man who had threatened Lydia and Alastair; instead, he was relieved the man no longer lived on ship.

"If you're done playing with your musical toy"—Alastair waved at the pianoforte—"which you play spectacularly well, by the way, then come to bed."

The words, spoken in a bored aristocratic drawl, had his wood up and ready in seconds. Damn, how this man affected him. He was across the galley and in Alastair's arms in two strides. Their lips crashed together hard, until they pulled back and gentled the kiss. Rhain delved in with his tongue and no finesse.

He wanted this man and wanted him now. The urgency was surprising, since they'd made slow, thorough love that morning, but his desire was undeniable in its potency.

"I want you. Here. Now."

Alastair pulled back, eyes wide. "Here?"

Rhain nodded and tried to pull the whipcord, tough man back into his arms, but Alastair backed out of the galley, shaking his head. "No,

Rhain. The place smells like hundreds of unwashed seamen; come to our cabin."

Their cabin, the captain's cabin, was now the captain's and Rhain's cabin. His few daily required items fit in with plenty of space to spare, and they'd rubbed along quite well for the past week. He had hopes of their liaison continuing in that fashion for a long time to come.

"I want you in a sweet-smelling place, with soft sheets, fresh air from large open windows, and at least three lanterns illuminating that perfect body of yours."

Through the entirety of that last sentence, Alastair slowly backed down the hall toward the stairs to the main deck, and Rhain slowly followed him, liking the idea of making love in their cabin. Although he would not give up on his new fantasy of fucking in the galley, he would save that for another day.

They barely made it to the cabin and got the door locked before he pounced on his pirate. He dipped down and lifted Alastair over his shoulder, then launched them both at the bed.

Alastair wheezed. "No need to go all Viking on me. I fully intend to offer up my arse for you." He landed on the bed. "Ooufff!"

Rhain took off his own clothes with more speed than finesse and heard a button ping somewhere on the floor. His breeches refused to cooperate with his passion-clumsy fingers. "Damnation."

Alastair scooted to the head of the bed and sat there, fully clothed, watching the show. "Well, if I'd known playing a few ditties on the pianoforte would work you up thusly, I would have unpacked the thing myself before we ever left London."

Laughing, he gave up on the last button and just pulled his breeches down, which required a bit of wiggling.

His lover watched the entire show.

When completely nude, he climbed onto the bed and started work on Alastair's clothing. "You know, this would go much faster if you helped."

"But it feels so much better when you slip my clothes off."

He had to admit it was delightful to reveal skin inch by inch as he uncovered his pirate, licking here and there, eliciting tantalizing moans as he went.

Soon they were lying side by side, caressing and stroking. Alastair leaned in for a slow kiss, their lips barely brushing. Hard to imagine such a gentle gesture could have Rhain so close to coming. He moved away and took a few deep breaths to control his lust. "Good God, what you do to me."

"There is much more I want to do to you. Are you up for it, my love?"

At that, he turned and looked at Alastair. "Do you want to fuck me? I've been meaning to ask, but we… I always am so, well, mindless that I forget. I'll admit it is not my favorite thing, but I'd be happy to…with you."

Alastair leaned over him and kissed him again. "Although the thought has lots of potential that we can explore at a later date, right now I want you to fuck me. Are you amenable to that?"

Reaching up and flipping them both over so that Alastair lay under him, he said, "Bloody hell, yes! I'm amenable to fucking your sweet arse."

ALASTAIR CLENCHED AND then relaxed the muscles in his arse as Rhain slid one oil-slicked finger into him. The look on his lover's face was so serious at this moment, he worried he wasn't enjoying himself. "Hurry up the preparation, will you. I want you to fuck me. Now. Hard. Until I can feel you every time I sit down tomorrow."

Rhain groaned and slid in another, and shortly after, a third finger. God, the stretch felt so wonderful, and now Rhain's expression was one of lust, not worry.

The man had been too contrite since returning to the ship where he belonged. Alastair had done all he could to convince him no one maintained any sour feelings for what transpired. Of course it made sense to try and make a plot of land turn a profit. It was admirable he tried so hard, against so many odds. But the boy was bullheaded for sure, and it would take time for him to forgive himself.

"I'm more than ready, love. Fuck me, now. I need to feel you moving that big lovely cock inside me until I wake every last man and woman on this ship with my cries."

"Well, you are rather voluble tonight." Smiling, he removed his fingers.

The abrupt loss stung, but then there was something filling his empty hole that made up for no fingers.

"Oh, yes. Yes!"

"Alastair, you are so goddamn hot. So tight." The words were squeezed off, and Rhain stopped moving, head tipped back, weight held up by two muscular arms. "God, you feel so good."

Once seated deep, the infuriating man did not move. He opened his eyes and looked at Alastair, the whiskey depths showing more emotion than he had seen there before. What was with his lover tonight? Was the damn pianoforte that important to him?

He bucked that desirable, large body, trying to motivate his lover into action. When that didn't inspire the wanted response, he said, "Move, damn you."

Rhain smiled again and then started a slow rhythm that was near enchanting. In, out, in, out. Their gazes locked on each other. Rhain reached down and kissed him, gently, oh-so-sweetly.

The intensity was almost too much. He wanted to look away but couldn't. After only a few moments, he was ready to spend. Clenching teeth to hold back the climax, he lost the battle at Rhain's words whispered in that beloved, rough baritone.

"I love you, my dear pirate. I will love you until the day I breathe my last breath. I will then love you forever after that. You are my soul, my life, my world. Say you will stay with me to the end of our days."

Alastair, beyond words, cried out loud enough to wake creatures at the depths of the ocean. His climax ripped sensation from every part of his body and focused it on a euphoric wave that swept him into oblivion for what felt like hours but most surely was mere seconds.

When he landed back in this world, Rhain had finished his own climax and was in the process of collapsing over him, his sweaty body pressing Alastair into the bedding.

They lay there for a long while, Alastair running his fingers through Rhain's hair. He liked the wavy locks in this longer style. It made him seem somewhat disreputable.

"Say it again."

"Hmmm?"

"You heard me. Say it."

"What, that I love you?" he lifted his head and gently kissed Alastair's lips. "With all my being."

Alastair smiled. "I think I want you to say that every day. At least three times a day."

"With pleasure, my love."

There should be a way to capture and sell the way he felt right then. If there were, he would be a wealthy man five times over. "My answer is yes, by the way."

"Truly?"

He nodded.

Rhain placed their foreheads together and sighed. "Good. Because I think I would expire on the spot if you said no."

"Such a dramatic reaction. Surely you are made of sturdier stuff than that."

"I'm not at all certain any longer. Wait here. I have something for you." Rhain disentangled them, leaving an ache in his body that was more from regret at no longer being joined than from any real discomfort. He watched the strong nude man hunting for something in a drawer.

"I found this in one of the crates when on the island. I'd almost forgotten about it. But when I found it, I knew that if I ever saw you again, I would ask you to take me back, and I would give you this." He placed in Alastair's hand a very small box that looked like a miniature sea locker with gold filigree tacked to its surface.

He looked at Rhain, who appeared to be about fifteen years old at the moment.

Inside the box lay a simple large gold-and-green bauble. He could already tell the thing would cost more than a purser's yearly salary.

"My father's emerald cravat pin. It was a gift from Mother; he wore it at their wedding. My mother's wedding band was in here as well; gave that one to Lydia. I, uh…" The man blushed.

Alastair loved that look on his bold, take-charge lover.

"I thought you could have this made into a ring for your ear. Perhaps secure it somehow to this one." He reached up and traced a gentle touch on Alastair's gold ring in his ear. "I would be honored if you would wear it."

He asked, thinking he knew the answer, but needing it said anyway, "And where will we live, Rhain?"

"For now, here on your boat."

He shook his head, unable to ignore the insult to his fine *Hurricane*, and corrected Rhain again, "Ship. She is a ship, Rhain."

The boy only grinned, then said, his voice low and suspiciously moist, "It doesn't matter to me where we live as long as I'm with you, for the rest of our lives, my pirate. I love you. I need you by my side. Will you have me?"

Alastair dropped the box and reached for his matelot.

The End

Other Titles by Stephanie Lake
The SECOND CHANCE Series
His Midshipman
His Second Chance
His Pirate

Contemporary romance
Thom's Desires

With Jules Radcliffe
Florian's Garden

A peek at His Second Chance by Stephanie Lake.

Viscount Randall Blair wants a second chance at love with his long-lost Lieutenant David Wedgewood. Only one problem: he's engaged to David's sister.

London, July 1784

I can do this.

Randall turned the phaeton into Hyde Park, then looked at Prudence. She was lovely—no, she was beautiful. Raven hair, flashing chocolate eyes, and ebony eyelashes that defied the late-afternoon sun. Include a petite frame and creamy, pale skin that had probably never been forced to suffer sunshine—even now her face was shaded by a beribboned hat—and that equaled beauty. Add in her wicked wit, and he thought he really could marry the chit. And be, if not happy, at least content with the fact he had followed the correct path.

He teased his favorite pair of bays into a smart trot along the packed-dirt lane, settling behind a landau carrying a smartly dressed couple and two red-haired boys, twins, perhaps. He waved back at the boys and enjoyed Prudence's seamless, sarcastic commentary. Her drollness was more than likely the reason she was still unwed at five and twenty, even being the daughter of an earl. But that suited Randall just fine. He loved a sharp, acerbic mind.

Yes, they would do nicely together.

"...and then, when my aunt careened down the bank, she knocked down two footmen and a speckled hound. I told her the whole scene resembled a game of bowls, and I suggested we all roll down the hill and try to knock down glass bottles; I was only ten at the time. All of us siblings and cousins spent the rest of the day getting grass stains on our best Sunday clothes. But Aunt Celia stopped crying and actually did a few more tumbles down the hill herself." The perfect light tinkling of laughter came from perfectly tinted lips, with perfect timing.

An elderly matron, riding in the back of another landau, smiled approvingly at them. Randall's chest swelled. Yes, Prudence would make him a first-rate viscountess. His aunt had made an excellent recommendation for a wife.

He could do this. Yes, he could.

"Oh, Lord Blair. Look." She pointed toward the crowded park, where dozens of strolling and riding London denizens enjoyed the waning rays of sunshine. "My brother, David." She turned and looked at him with a radiance he'd never seen in her always perfectly contained features. She was so beautiful at that moment, he almost thought he could love this one woman. Almost.

"He is my favorite sibling but has been away oh so long." She half stood and waved at a dark young man dressed in a naval officer's uniform and riding a smart-looking dappled gray. The young man reined in to trot toward them. Firm, fine thighs controlled the spirited horse while posting. Magnificent

Randall swallowed his lust. It would not do to admire men any longer. He was to marry soon. He would simply have to change his tastes.

Prudence gave a little squeal. She actually squealed with excitement as her brother stopped his horse and reached over to take her hand to his lips.

He almost laughed at her unexpected giddiness, but then the brother raised his head and pinned him with a glare and... Bloody hell. No!

Perfect features, so like his sister's—raven hair, flashing gunmetal-black eyes with lashes too long to believe, angry winged brows, and the only evidence this man was human and not some fallen angel was a slight spattering of freckles across the skin of his straight, flawless nose. Skin he remembered tasting. Warm and salty.

All the blood fled from his face for lower regions.

Slight musk that grew stronger the closer his lips had come to... Oh God! Bloody hell. I had Prudence's brother.

Bloody damn hell. I had my cock up Prudence's brother's arse.

More than once!

Hands shaking, sweat beading between shoulder blades and running down his back, his vision of smooth, young, naked skin turned away from an ideal week five years ago and back to harsh reality…to judgmental eyes, the exact shape as Prudence's. He should have known. No wonder he thought she was beautiful—she looked so much like her brother. A brother he at one time had been half in love with.

He closed his eyes, unable to bear the condemnation from a face he remembered in the throes of passion—mouth open, sighs and moans issuing from perfect lips. And between the times of passion, a wicked wit.

He should have known.

He was doomed.

He could not force air into burning, constricted lungs.

His surroundings dimmed.

The phaeton surged forward. Prudence screamed.

Just as quickly, the bay horses stopped, tossing their heads and snorting. David had one lead.

"Release the reins, Lord Blair." Snapped out like an enemy flag on an angry wind. "Let…the reins…drop!"

Randall pried his numb fingers away from the tortured leather and felt his future plans die with each extracted digit. He took shallow breaths, trying to feed air-starved lungs. What would David do? What did he want? He knew everything, for God's sake.

He had fucked the man.

Groaning, a torturous sound, he raked his hands over his face. The abrasive pull did not help his composure. This cannot be happening.

"My lord, are you unwell?"

He nodded at her concern, thought better of it, then shook his head instead.

David smoothly tied off the reins and set the brake before Randall had his breathing under control. "A word with you, sir. You placed my sister's life in danger, and I intend to give you a bit of my mind."

"Oh, David, no. Lord Blair is very competent and has never before put me in danger, and I am sure…"

Snapping ebony eyes stilled her attempt at rescue. Randall was doomed, his future in ruins. He scrubbed his face again, resetting his features, hoping to calm chaotic emotions as well. "He is quite right, my lady. We will be but a moment, I'm sure. And a gentle set-down will likely do my humility good."

"Oh, David, don't."

David raised a hand, and it carried as much command as Ol' George himself.

Randall slid from the seat and followed two broad and very stiff shoulders. Shoulders he had last seen leaving his bed for an appointment with some solicitor or other. Shoulders on the man who had not, as promised, returned.

They reached a secluded spot under a large, stately oak and were only thirty feet or so from the phaeton, but there was one thing he had to know and it could wait no longer. "David. You disappeared. I tried to find you. I feared—"

David spun on his heels, flinging words along with spittle. "What are your intentions for my sister?"

So much for sentimentality. He straightened his back and stood to his full, intimidating height, which was approximately four inches taller than his accuser. "I have asked her to be my wife, and she accepted. The family is excited, and the banns have been sent, if not yet read. The family is quite thrilled with this match, it would seem."

David grabbed Randall's cravat and tightened his grip, making further comment impossible.

"You will not marry my sister, you bloody sodomite."

He wiped moisture from his face and then applied a warning pressure to the long, elegant fingers cutting off his breath. The constricted cloth eased. "And who is calling me a bloody sodomite, Midshipman David…Smith, was it?"

David let go and shook his head. At least he had the decency to look embarrassed about using a fake name five years ago, but his expression was no less murderous. "There is a difference in that I am not trying to force my unnatural proclivities on an unsuspecting lady. I will not let you ruin her life."

"Ruin? She will be a viscountess. She and I get along smashingly. How will that—"

"And do you plan to fuck every young military man on leave? Break her heart? Give her nothing of yourself? Pass on some disease?"

Randall turned away from the accusation that hit a little too close to home. But the new perspective was just as disconcerting—instead of an irate protective brother, there was lovely Prudence leaning half off her perch, taking in everything. Fortunately, they were too far away for her to hear. He turned back to the irate brother.

"I will not let you destroy her with your unnatural appetites."

"And what will you do to stop me? Call me out? Under what pretense, pray tell? That I'm queer? And what evidence will you use?" He chanced much when he leaned in and ran a finger down David's smooth, freshly shaven cheek. "That you know firsthand since you enjoyed my cock in this pretty little mouth…" He ran his finger to David's full wide lips. "And in your—"

David flung off the offending caress. "You son of a... I will not let you do this. There is no way you can make her happy."

"She seems quite happy to have me as husband. Likes my fair hair, she says. Says we will make pretty babies. And maybe, with a little convincing, you and I could—" He knew he'd pushed too far. He expected the punch. However, he prepared for a facer. One short punch to the gut, a lightning bolt to his jaw, and the conversation was over.

The world spun for a few seconds.

"David!" Prudence yelled.

"Leave my sister alone. Tell everyone you made a mistake. That the two of you will not suit. I will console the family."

Randall shook his head. Damn. David had grown into a fine, strong, sneaky bastard in the past five years. Pain throbbed in his ears as he rubbed his jaw. No blood, nothing broken. And fortunately, his stomach only received a glancing blow.

The swish of silk stopped Randall's retort.

"Oh, my dear, sweet Lord Blair." Featherlight touches assessed his wholeness. Then she glared at her brother. "David, what are you about? This is my betrothed. He did nothing untoward and does not deserve this treatment."

Randall grinned over Prudence's shoulder, knowing he had just gained martyr status.

David turned a sickly color of purple, then grabbed Prudence's arm and dragged her, protesting all the way, to the phaeton and the gray tethered behind.

He let them go; it was almost worth having to walk back home, watching Prudence attempt to scramble out of the vehicle, and David repeatedly pulling her back in as he drove away.

Almost worth walking. He stopped to pry a stone out of his soft leather sole. Unfortunately, strolling would give him too much time to think, and his current disposition was more suited to February's perpetual haze than today's perfect sunny weather.

Yes, the walk would take too long, too long indeed. His thoughts turned to the flashing black eyes of the man who had lied, loved, and then disappeared.

About Stephanie Lake

Stephanie Lake is the pen name for a husband/wife team who enjoy writing historical M/M (gay) romance with happy endings and steamy middles. We hope you enjoyed *His Pirate*, the second book in the *Second Chance* series. If you liked *His Pirate*, please leave a review on the site where you purchased the book or on Goodreads. Thanks! :)

We'd love to hear from you, so check out our website and Facebook for contact info at:

https://sites.google.com/site/stephanielakeauthorcom/home

https://www.facebook.com/StephanieLakeRomance

Sign up for our newsletter for a free read in the Second Chance series, *His Midshipmen.*

Stephanie Lake joined forces with Jules Radcliffe, another author of queer historical fiction, to produce a monthly newsletter with news and updates on what we're doing, plus competitions and giveaways.

http://julesradcliffe.us10.list-manage.com/subscribe?
u=076191e5c5ec5e9c6bfd29696&id=c42fdeb897

YOU'VE REACHED

"THE END!"

BUY THIS AND MORE TITLES AT

www.eXcessica.com

eXcessica's Yahoo Groups

groups.yahoo.com/group/eXcessica/

eXcessica's Forum

www.eXcessica.com/forum

Check us out for updates about eXcessica books!

WRITE A REVIEW!

Readers in the age of ebooks are in control of separating the good from the bad, the wheat from the chaff.

Please take a moment to leave a review were you purchased this book and express your opinion, however lengthy or brief.

You can also plaster your reviews on social media or other book review sites.

Make your voice count! Your opinion will help other readers make their future purchasing decisions in regards to print and ebooks.

Made in the USA
Middletown, DE
29 May 2019